MANDIE
AND THE

Mandie Mysteries

Mandie's Cookbook
Mandie and Joe's Christmas Surprise

9606

MANDIE

AND THE
SCHOOLHOUSE'S
SECRET

Lois Gladys Leppard

BETHANY HOUSE PUBLISHERS
MINNEAPOLIS, MINNESOTA 55438

Mandie and the Schoolhouse's Secret
Lois Gladys Leppard

Library of Congress Catalog Card Number
96–25281

ISBN 1–55661–553–1

Published by Bethany House Publishers
A Ministry of Bethany Fellowship, Inc.
11300 Hampshire Avenue South
Minneapolis, Minnesota 55438

Printed in the United States of America.

In Memory of My Dear,
Long-Time Friend,
Margaret E. Olson of Minneapolis,
a Faithful Supporter.

About the Author

LOIS GLADYS LEPPARD has been a Federal Civil Service employee in various countries around the world. She makes her home in South Carolina.

The stories of her own mother's childhood are the basis for many of the incidents incorporated in this series.

Contents

"Happy is the man that findeth wisdom,
and the man that getteth understanding:
For the merchandise of it is better
than the merchandise of silver,
and the gain thereof than fine gold."
Proverbs 3:13–14

Chapter 1 / Things to Come

Mandie Shaw kept nodding, in spite of herself, as Uncle Ned drove the rig down the mountain road in the late-evening darkness. She would have liked to stay longer at the Woodards, but her grandmother had sent Uncle Ned, her father's old Cherokee friend, to bring her home. And now that she was on the way, she was eager to get to Mrs. Taft's house. So much had happened during her visit with the Woodards. And Mandie wanted to talk about everything with her grandmother.

"I don't really want to go to sleep," Mandie said, as she straightened up beside Uncle Ned and yawned. "But I'll sure be glad when we get to Grandmother's." Snowball, her cat, was curled up asleep in her lap.

"We hurry, Papoose," Uncle Ned said with a smile. "Soon there. Then Papoose sleep."

"Oh, but I'll have so many things to tell Grandmother I'll probably be up all night," Mandie said.

She touched the metal box on the floorboard with her foot. Her father's legal papers were in it, and she needed Uncle John to look over everything. Her father had died the year before, and his brother John had married Mandie's mother. But she didn't know when she would see Uncle John because she was going to her grandmother's house in Asheville, the town where she went to school.

"Grandmother not allow all night," Uncle Ned said. "Papoose must sleep tonight." He guided the horse down the narrow dirt road.

"I think she'll be interested in hearing about what happened," Mandie said. "And I'm anxious to know whether we're going to President McKinley's funeral or not." Her blue eyes filled with tears as she thought about the big, friendly man. She had gone with her grandmother to his second inauguration that spring. They had been his guests in the White House. A demented man had shot him the week before and he had died this morning—September 14, 1901, at 2:15 A.M.

"Long way," Uncle Ned said. "Maybe not time."

When they arrived at Mrs. Taft's huge house, she was waiting for them in the parlor. Uncle Ned let Mandie out at the front door and went on to the back to put the rig and horse up for the night. Ella, the maid, answered the door. As soon as the door opened, Snowball jumped down from Mandie's arms and raced off toward the kitchen.

"Grandmother!" Mandie exclaimed as she rushed to her in the parlor. Tears streamed down Mandie's face.

Mrs. Taft quickly rose from her chair by the fireplace and embraced her. "I'm glad you're back, dear," she said as she pushed back the hood on

Mandie's cloak and smoothed her blond hair.

Mandie hurriedly removed her cloak and hung it on the hall tree. She tried to control her emotions so she could speak, as she pulled a stool over to her grandmother's chair and sat down. "Grandmother, it's all so terrible," she said in a choked voice. "President McKinley was such a nice man, and now he's gone."

"Yes, dear," Mrs. Taft said. "It's a shame we have to lose our president."

Mandie looked up at the woman and asked, "Are we going to his funeral?" She wiped her face with a lacy handkerchief from her pocket.

"No, dear, I'm not sure what they're planning for him, but it would be useless for us to try and go," Mrs. Taft replied. "There will be so many people there, and there's nothing we can do."

"I suppose so," Mandie reluctantly agreed.

Uncle Ned came to the doorway and spoke, "Horse put up and rig in barn."

"Do come on in and sit down, Uncle Ned," Mrs. Taft told him.

"We are not going to President McKinley's funeral," Mandie told Uncle Ned as he sat down nearby.

"No, not necessary," the old man agreed.

Mandie turned back to her grandmother and asked, "Then, why did you send Uncle Ned for me a day earlier than we had planned?"

"I decided you needed to get back and get over this bad news about President McKinley before you go back to school Monday," Mrs. Taft replied.

"Grandmother, I just remembered something," Mandie said quickly. "You know my stepsister, Irene. Well, she has the measles bad, and Joe and I were both around her without knowing what she had. Dr. Woodard said there's a possibility we could catch the measles from her.''

"Oh, dear,'' Mrs. Taft said, plainly worried. "What will we do? I think you'd better stay here for a few days until we see whether you develop any symptoms. If you go back to school and suddenly come down with the measles, all the girls there would be at risk.''

"Oh, Grandmother,'' Mandie said with a big sigh. "I don't really think I'm going to get the measles. You see, the house was on fire when we found Irene, and Dr. Woodard is hoping that killed the germs.''

"What? The Woodards' house?'' Mrs. Taft asked, alarmed at the idea.

"Oh no, my father's house,'' Mandie said. "You see, Irene was inside the house, really bad off with the measles, when Joe and I broke in after the fire started. She would have died from the fire if we hadn't rescued her. And my father's house would have burned down.''

"Amanda!'' Mrs. Taft said. "Please begin at the beginning. I have no idea what you're talking about.''

"Well, you see, it was like this . . .'' Mandie began. "Joe and I kept watching the house, and we saw someone peep out the window, but we couldn't get anyone to come to the door. Then we could tell the house was on fire, so we broke out a window and went inside and found Irene, completely unconscious, lying on some quilts near the fire in the fireplace. And Dr. Woodard is not sure she will recover.''

"Oh, dear,'' Mrs. Taft murmured as she listened.

"And Joe and I found this metal box under the floor where the fire had burned a hole—" she quickly interrupted herself and turned to Uncle Ned. "Did you bring the box in?"

"Box in hall with Papoose's bags," Uncle Ned assured her.

"A metal box?" Mrs. Taft asked.

"Yes, ma'am," Mandie answered. "And it's full of my father's legal papers. Joe said one paper is his will and that my father willed the house to me. I'm going to get Uncle John to go through everything. And there are photographs in it, too. Uncle John will be able to identify the people in the pictures, I hope." She stood up as she added, "I'll go get it and show you everything."

"No, no, Amanda, it's late, and we all need to get to bed," Mrs. Taft told her. "And we have other problems. If you have been exposed to measles, then I'll have to send Hilda over to stay with the Mannings until we're sure you are safe. She has already gone to bed for the night."

"I'm sorry, Grandmother," Mandie said.

"I'm sorry you've been exposed to such a disease," Mrs. Taft replied. She looked at Uncle Ned and asked, "Would you be able to stay long enough to get a message to the Mannings to see if they will keep Hilda a few days? And if they will, I'd appreciate it if you could drive Hilda over there. Hilda trusts you, and you know how shy she is with some people."

"I take her," the old man replied. "I be glad. I go home when sun rises Monday."

"Thank you, Uncle Ned," Mrs. Taft said as she rose.

Hilda was a girl Mandie and her friend Celia had

found hiding in the schoolhouse, and Mrs. Taft had given her a home. The girl was unpredictable and didn't seem able to talk. She was afraid of almost everyone.

As the old man stood, Mandie got up from her stool and said, "I'm glad you're staying 'til Monday, Uncle Ned, since I have to stay here a few days."

As the three started to leave the room, Mrs. Taft paused and said, "You might like to know, Amanda, that I am having electricity and a furnace put into your schoolhouse, but I understand it is creating a mess with the men boring holes in the walls and floors."

"Oh, this is going to be interesting," Mandie said, smiling. "Grandmother, please let me go back to school in time to see what they're doing. I've never seen anyone put in electricity or one of those furnaces."

Mrs. Taft smiled at her and said, "They'll still be there when you get back. This is going to take quite a long time to do. Now let's all go to our rooms and get some sleep. Uncle Ned, Ella made the usual room upstairs ready for you."

"Thank, ma'am," the old man said smiling.

"And, Amanda, be sure you go to bed and get some sleep. We'll be having breakfast at seven o'clock like usual," her grandmother reminded her as they went out into the hallway.

"Yes, ma'am," Mandie said, hurrying toward her bags and the box near the hall tree. Snowball came running to her, and she picked him up.

"I help Papoose carry," Uncle Ned said. He stooped to sling his own bag over his shoulder, then picked up Mandie's bags.

She grabbed the metal box. "I'll carry this one,

Uncle Ned," Mandie said, smiling up at him.

The old man smiled back at her and said, "I understand, Papoose."

As they started up the steps, Mrs. Taft went ahead of them.

"Good night, now, and I'll see y'all downstairs at seven," Mrs. Taft reminded Mandie and Uncle Ned. "Amanda, you let me know if you start feeling bad."

"Oh, I will, Grandmother, but don't worry about me. I'm just not going to get the measles," Mandie said as her grandmother went on down the hallway. Uncle Ned pushed open Mandie's bedroom door and deposited her bags inside.

"Good night, Papoose," he told her as he continued down the hall.

"Good night, Uncle Ned. See you in the morning," Mandie replied as she closed the door and set Snowball down. She noticed a sandbox in the corner. Her grandmother never forgot about her cat.

A fire in the fireplace threw out warmth, and the room was comfortable after the chilly ride through the mountains. Mandie set the metal box down near the bed and quickly found her nightclothes in her bag. She put them on as Snowball jumped on the bed and curled up to sleep. Then she sat down on the low stool in front of the fire and thought about the events of the last few days.

"I'm not going to get the measles," she said to herself with a big sigh. "I have to stay here and waste time when I could be back at school telling Celia everything that happened."

Then she remembered what her grandmother had said about installing electricity and a furnace in the school. She was glad her grandmother had agreed to help out when Miss Hope and Miss Prudence were about to close up the school. And now her grandmother was behind all this modernization! She wasn't sure she'd like living in a place that had those light bulbs that temporarily blinded you if you looked directly at them. And if that furnace in the schoolhouse turned out to be like the one in Davenport's Department Store downtown, it would be chugging, banging, and blowing out steam all day and all night. Her grandmother didn't have such a thing in her own house. Why was she having one put in the schoolhouse?

"And I'm missing out on all this—seeing how they put in electricity and the furnace. I don't know how it's done," she mumbled to herself as the fire began making her sleepy.

She knew she should get in bed before she went to sleep on the stool. She stood up, stretched, yawned, and then blew out the lamp on the mantelpiece. Sitting on the side of the bed, she dislodged Snowball, and he meowed angrily as he moved around looking for another spot to curl up.

"You were in my place, Snowball. You just stay over there on your own side," Mandie told the cat as she reached for the lamp on the night table and extinguished the light.

Once in bed her thoughts seemed to be on a merry-go-round. A little bit of everything kept racing through her mind. She was anxious to hear about Irene. She wanted to know if Joe came down with the measles. She wanted to ask Uncle John about the legal papers.

"Oh, shucks, shucks, shucks!" she exclaimed as she turned over to the other side and buried her face in the pillow. "I've got to go to sleep. I've got to get up and be ready for breakfast at seven."

After turning and tossing for a while, Mandie finally began dropping off to sleep. Then suddenly the bed springs moved as someone slipped in on the other side of the bed. She came wide awake and jumped out to stand on the floor while she felt for the matches and lit the lamp. The wick flickered. There was Hilda in her bed.

"Oh, Hilda, you can't sleep here," Mandie tried to explain. "You see, I've been exposed to measles, and Grandmother wouldn't want you around me. Now you have to go back to your bed." She threw back the covers.

Hilda didn't seem to understand what she was saying. The girl looked up at her and didn't move. Mandie knew it was hard to get through to Hilda sometimes. She went and opened the door to the hallway and came back to the bed.

"Go back to your room, Hilda," Mandie said, pointing to the door.

Hilda shook her head and didn't move. But Snowball, disturbed from his sleep, meowed loudly and jumped down to the floor. Hilda immediately followed him and picked him up. She held him tightly in her arms and smiled at Mandie.

Mandie knew Hilda loved Snowball, so she said, "You can take him to your room." She motioned for Hilda to leave the room.

Hilda frowned as she looked at Mandie, then finally started toward the door. Mandie followed her to the hallway.

"Go back to bed now, Hilda," she told the girl. "I'll see you in the morning."

Hilda smiled and, holding tightly on to Snowball, turned suddenly and ran down the hallway to her room. Mandie went back inside her room and turned the latch on the door.

"I sure wouldn't want Hilda to get the measles," she mumbled to herself as she put out the lamp and jumped back into bed.

The next thing Mandie knew, someone was knocking on her door. She rubbed her sleepy eyes and turned over to look in that direction. Then she remembered that she had locked the door.

"Missy 'Manda, I needs to git in and light de fire," Annie, the upstairs maid, called to her.

Mandie rolled out of bed and hurried to open the door.

"Good morning, Annie," Mandie greeted her as she stepped back to allow the young girl to enter.

Mandie grabbed her robe from the foot of her bed and put it on. It was chilly in the room without a fire going.

"Mawnin', Missy 'Manda," Annie replied as she set to work in front of the fireplace adding kindling to the dead ashes and sticking newspaper in between. She struck a match, touched it to the paper, and the fire roared into flames. She stood up and watched for a minute. "Guess dat oughta do it."

"Thanks, Annie," Mandie said, hovering near the fireplace. "I suppose I'll be staying here for a few days. I was exposed to measles, so you may not want to get near me."

"Oh no, Missy 'Manda," the girl exclaimed. "Measles, dey kin be dangerous. I done had 'em long time ago. Cain't ketch 'em agin, dey say."

"Well, I hope not," Mandie replied. "But I don't really believe I'm going to get the measles." She told the girl about how she and Joe rescued Irene from the fire.

"Naw, you ain't gwine git no measles. Dat fire done kilt 'em," Annie agreed.

"Grandmother said they've started putting in electricity and a furnace at the schoolhouse, and I'm real anxious to get back over there to see how they do it," Mandie told the girl. "Have you been over there for anything?"

"Lawsy mercy, yes, Missy 'Manda," Annie said. "Dey jes' got de biggest mess I ever seed. Holes all over de place, in de walls and in de floors."

"Do you know if they made holes in Celia's and my room?" Mandie asked.

"No, dat I don't be knowin'. Miz Taft she sent dis note to dat Miz Prudence, and I only went to de room where she work wid all de papers and things," Annie explained. "But I seed holes in de hallway and in her room."

"Well, I sure hope they cover the holes back up," Mandie said.

"I hears tell dat Miz Taft, she gwine have one of dem tellegaphones put in de school, too," Annie added.

"A telephone in the school?" Mandie asked. "What good will a telephone be in the school? We don't have anyone to call up on it."

"Oh, but she also gwine put one in dis heah house, she say," Annie said.

"She is?" Mandie exclaimed. "Then, I suppose she'll use the one here to call up the one in the schoolhouse."

"Dat's right. She say she won't hafta git in de rig and go over dere so much den," Annie explained. "Missy 'Manda, I ain't never seed one of dem things. Do dey be dangerous?"

Mandie laughed and said, "No, Annie, I've seen

them in other places. You just pick up the thing called the receiver, which hangs on the side, and put it to your ear, and there's another piece that you talk into and you can hear whoever is on the other telephone."

"But you don't be in de same place? How dat be?" Annie asked.

"I'm not sure, Annie, but there are wires connected to the telephone, and the wires run on the poles down the street to the other telephone," Mandie explained. "Haven't you ever noticed those poles downtown with wires on the top of them?"

Annie shrugged and said, "I seed 'em, but I thought dat dey be fo' de light bulbs whut some people put in de house or de store."

"That's right. Everything goes on the same poles—I think," Mandie told her, not quite sure herself how it all worked.

"Sounds not real to me," Annie said. "Now I got to git de other fires lit." She went toward the door. She looked around the room and asked, "Where dat white cat at?"

"Oh, he's in Hilda's room," Mandie explained. "That's why I had the door locked, to keep Hilda from coming in here again. Grandmother is going to send her to the Mannings 'til she sees whether I get the measles or not. Hilda came in here last night and I let her take Snowball with her to her room."

"I go light her fire and see dat Snowball be all right," Annie said. "And I got all de rest to light, too. Yours be the first one today."

"Thank you, Annie," Mandie said as the girl went out the door. "Snowball doesn't have a sandbox in Hilda's room, and I'm supposed to stay away from Hilda. So maybe you could bring him back to me."

"I'll do dat," Annie said as she went down the hallway.

As Mandie started to close the door, she spotted her white cat running toward her. She waited for him, and he rushed through the door and straight to his sandbox.

"Well, you're a pretty smart cat," Mandie said as she closed the door. She walked over to the huge wardrobe and opened it. She kept a few clothes in it because she visited her grandmother every chance she had to get away from school, which was only a few blocks away.

"Well, today's Sunday, but I doubt Grandmother will allow me to go to church, so I'll just put on this navy dress. It's warm and comfortable," she said to herself as she pulled the dress down from the hanger.

As she put on the dress and buttoned the bodice, she pouted to herself, "It's probably going to be a boring day today."

But Mandie was wrong. The day would be full of surprises.

Chapter 2 / An Eventful Day

As Mandie sat at the breakfast table with her grandmother and Uncle Ned, Mrs. Taft made the announcement Mandie had expected. "We won't be going to church today," she said. "We don't want to take a chance on spreading measles. And Annie is keeping Hilda in her room. They are taking their breakfast up there. Maybe the Mannings will agree to keep her for a few days."

Uncle Ned spoke up, "I eat. I go to Mannings."

"I sure hope I don't get the measles," Mandie said as she drank her coffee. Setting her cup down she added, "I don't really think I will."

"It's better to accept it as a possibility, dear," Mrs. Taft told her as she buttered a biscuit. "But, of course, I certainly trust you won't."

As soon as they were finished with the meal, Uncle Ned left to drive over to the Mannings' house.

Mandie went to read in the sun parlor. Snowball curled up asleep on the carpet in the sunshine coming through the long window. Mrs. Taft sat in front of the fireplace, restlessly awaiting Uncle Ned's return.

When Uncle Ned came back he did not have good news. Mrs. Taft motioned to him to come in and sit down.

"Mannings say sorry they leave town today. Go to daughter for week," he told Mrs. Taft as he sat in a chair nearby.

"Oh dear, what will we do?" Mrs. Taft said, disappointed with the message.

"I take Hilda to my house, see Sallie," Uncle Ned suggested.

"Well, I just don't know, Uncle Ned," Mrs. Taft said. "What if she decided to run away out there in the country? We might never find her."

"Sallie watch," the old man told her. "I go to my house now if Hilda go, too."

"But you had not planned on going home until tomorrow," Mrs. Taft said.

"Only wait for tomorrow for John Shaw to come," Uncle Ned explained.

"For John Shaw to come? Is he coming here?" Mrs. Taft asked, surprised.

"I send message last night. Papoose want him to see metal box," the old man said, glancing at Mandie.

Mandie straightened up and said, "Uncle John is coming here? How do you know he's coming here?"

Uncle Ned smiled at her and said, "Brave follow us here last night. I tell him go tell John Shaw."

"I didn't see anyone follow us here," Mandie said.

Uncle Ned smiled again and said, "Brave follow

us all way from Woodards' house. Keep us safe at night. Papoose no see. Brave keep quiet and watch."

Mandie remembered then that the Cherokee Indians had their own system of doing things. Evidently Uncle Ned had the young man act as a bodyguard for them as they came through the dark mountain territory. He would have alerted Uncle Ned if he had seen any dangerous animals or any person who might want to harm them.

"Of course," Mandie said as she thought about it. "You always have someone watching out for us when I go with you places, don't you?"

"Most times," the old man replied.

"And you sent for Uncle John to come and look through the metal box I found," Mandie said with a big smile. "Thank you, Uncle Ned. I appreciate that."

Mrs. Taft looked at Mandie and said, "Yes, it's a good idea to get your uncle John to go through those papers. But what am I going to do about Hilda?"

"Grandmother, I think Sallie would watch her, and I imagine Hilda would enjoy visiting the Cherokee people," Mandie said.

Mrs. Taft looked at Uncle Ned and asked, "So you think Sallie wouldn't mind looking after Hilda? She can be a lot of trouble sometimes, so she has to be watched. You know how she likes to run away whenever she gets a chance."

"Sallie like see Hilda," Uncle Ned said. "Go to school with Sallie."

"Oh yes, they're using the new schoolhouse we built," Mandie said. "And Hilda might enjoy being in Mr. Riley O'Neal's classes. I'm sure he'd be interested in trying to teach Hilda, even if it would be only for a week or so."

Mrs. Taft took a deep breath and finally said, "Well, all right."

She looked at Uncle Ned and asked, "When do you plan on leaving?"

"Soon, when Hilda ready," Uncle Ned told her.

"I'll have to get some things together," Mrs. Taft said. She stood up and started for the door, saying, "I won't be long." Looking back, she told Mandie, "Amanda, you must remember to tell your uncle John when he gets here that you've been exposed to the measles."

"I will, Grandmother," Mandie promised.

Uncle Ned stood up as he said, "I get horse and wagon ready."

Mrs. Taft left the room and Mandie quickly rose to catch Uncle Ned's hand. "When are you coming back to see me? I can't go anywhere because of the measles danger," she told him.

Uncle Ned looked down at her and smiled as he squeezed her hand. "Soon," he said. "Soon. Go now." He hurried outside.

Mandie went to stand by the window as she heard Mrs. Taft and Hilda go out the front door. Uncle Ned pulled his wagon to the front and stopped at the steps. Hilda seemed excited as she got into the wagon and sat down.

"If only she could talk," Mandie said to herself as she watched her old friend drive the wagon toward the road. Hilda looked back and waved to Mrs. Taft on the porch.

Mandie went back to her chair and picked up her book as Mrs. Taft came inside and stopped by the doorway.

"I do hope Hilda will be all right," Mrs. Taft said.

"I'm sure she will be, Grandmother. You know, it looks to me like someone could teach her to talk if they really tried hard, and I imagine Mr. Riley O'Neal *will* try," Mandie said with a big smile.

"I'm just not sure Hilda is capable of learning. But, who knows? Someone might succeed in getting through to her," Mrs. Taft replied. "I'm going to Hilda's room now and put things in order. I'm afraid I had to pack so fast I left things in a mess."

"And I'm going to finish reading my book," Mandie said as she put her feet up on a footstool and got comfortable. She looked down at her cat, still sleeping on the carpet. "And I suppose Snowball will continue his nap."

"I'll be back down when it's time for the noon meal," Mrs. Taft promised as she went on down the hallway.

Mandie didn't get to read long before she heard a knock on the front door. She knew the servants had all gone to church, so she rushed to open the door. Uncle John was standing there smiling.

"Uncle John!" Mandie exclaimed and quickly looked beyond him to the buggy in the driveway to see if anyone else was there. "Mother didn't come?" she said, disappointed.

"No, not this time," Uncle John said as she stepped aside for him to enter the hallway. "She wanted to, but I didn't think she was strong enough after her illness to travel yet." He removed his coat and hat and hung them on the hall tree.

"Of course," Mandie agreed as she remembered the terrible sick spell her mother had gone through recently. She tiptoed to kiss her uncle on the cheek. "But I'm really glad to see you, Uncle John."

John Shaw embraced her and kissed the top of her head. "And I'm thankful you are in one piece after the experiences you and Joe had at his house, exposed to the measles and a fire, too."

"Come on in," Mandie told him as she led the way into the parlor. "Sit down, and I'll run upstairs and let Grandmother know you're here. And I'll get the metal box I found in my father's house."

John Shaw sat down near the fire while Mandie rushed up the staircase.

When Mandie returned to the parlor with the metal box, Mrs. Taft came behind her.

"Welcome," Mrs. Taft said, crossing the room to shake hands with him. He rose at her entrance. "I know you and Amanda have a lot to discuss, so I'll just leave you alone until time to eat. But please bring your bags in and set them out in the hall. As soon as the servants return from church someone will carry them up to your room for you."

"Thank you for the welcome. It's always a pleasure to visit here," he said with a big smile for the lady. "And I'll bring in my overnight case. I'll be returning home early in the morning."

"Oh, you must stay as long as you wish," Mrs. Taft told him. "And how is Elizabeth?" she inquired about her daughter, Mandie's mother.

"Getting along just fine," John replied as they stood in the middle of the parlor. "But I didn't think she should make the journey this time. She's got a long way to go before she's her old self again, I'm afraid."

"Yes, you did right," Mrs. Taft said. "Give her my love when you return home, and tell her I want her to take care of herself."

"That I will," he said.

Mandie stood there listening and wishing they would hurry and get over with the conversation. She had set the metal box down by the chair where John Shaw had been sitting and was eager for him to look at the contents.

Mrs. Taft glanced at her and said, "I'll be upstairs if you need me." Then, turning, she left the room.

"Let me get my bag from the buggy," he told her. "And I really need to put the horse away." He hesitated in the doorway.

"You don't have to do that," Mandie told him quickly. "Ben can take care of the horse. He should be back from church any time now. Grandmother and I didn't go to church because of the measles possibility. She even sent Hilda home with Uncle Ned this morning so she wouldn't catch it if I do come down with the measles." She paused and looked up at him. "Are you afraid you might catch the measles?"

"No, I don't believe so. I had the measles when I was small and, as far as I know, a person can't get the measles twice—at least I hope not. Now, I'll be right back," he told her as he went on down the hallway and out the front door.

Mandie stood in the doorway of the parlor until he came back inside with one bag, which he set by the hall tree. Then he rejoined her in the parlor. They sat in two chairs next to each other.

"I found this box under the floor of the front room in my father's house," Mandie said, sliding down to sit on a low footstool as she opened the lid of the box. "I don't know why my father put it in such a place."

"Oh, but that's common practice out in the country. Almost everyone keeps their legal papers and valuables in a metal box," Uncle John explained as he watched Mandie remove the top paper. "And they usually put it in a place where it won't be stolen or burned if there's a fire. Metal boxes are very important to country people and to a lot of people living in town."

"I'm not sure whether the box would have burned if we hadn't put out the fire in my father's house," Mandie said, holding up a legal document for him. "Joe said this is my father's will."

John Shaw took the paper and quickly read through it. "It is indeed your father's will, and it's a very important paper," he explained.

"Joe also said that paper gives me my father's house," Mandie continued, eagerly waiting for his reply.

"It certainly does," he replied. Then glancing up at her from the paper he added, "This needs to be recorded in the courthouse for Swain County as soon as possible so there won't be any question about your rights."

Mandie sighed and said, "Oh, Uncle John, how am I going to do that? We have a courthouse here in Asheville. Can't I just take it down to that courthouse?"

"No, that won't do at all," Uncle John explained. "You see, this is Buncombe County and this will was written in Swain County for property in that county, and your father also died in that county. Therefore, the paper has to be recorded there. I can act as your legal guardian, if you wish, and take care of all this. I know your mother should take care of this, but I can be appointed to handle your affairs since your mother is physically not able to do so right now." He looked at her as he waited for her reply.

"Oh, please do, Uncle John. I have no idea what to do if you don't take care of it for me," Mandie said eagerly. "And I know Mother would want you to do that, too."

"Then I'll take it with me when I leave here and, after I get home, I'll make the journey to Swain County Courthouse as soon as I can," he told her with a smile.

"Thanks, Uncle John," Mandie said, hurriedly taking the other papers out of the box for him to read. As she handed them to him, she said, "And, Uncle John, there are some old photographs in the bottom."

"I'll certainly be interested in looking at them after we get through all the papers," he told her as he looked over the next paper. "This is the deed to your father's property," he stated. As Mandie continued passing papers to him, he told her what each document was. "And this is the record of your father's marriage to Etta." He paused as he examined the contents of several envelopes. "And these are letters written to your father by your grandmother—"

Mandie interrupted as she snatched the papers from him. "Then, I have an idea of what was in those letters, and I don't want to read them right now," she said sadly. "My grandmother told my father that my mother didn't want to stay married to him, didn't she?" Tears glistened in her eyes as she clutched the papers.

"That's right," John Shaw acknowledged. "And since you know now that it was not so, and because you are on good terms with your grandmother, I agree we should just put those letters back in the box and ignore them, for the time being, anyway."

Mandie turned the box upside down, spilling out the balance of the contents. Then she quickly pushed the letters into the bottom of the empty box. *That is all over with*, she thought. There was nothing that could be done about it now. And her grandmother had told her long ago that she was sorry. So it was better for all concerned to ignore the letters now, as Uncle John suggested.

He had picked up some of the photographs Mandie had dumped from the box onto the floor, and as he showed one to Mandie he exclaimed, "This is your grandmother Talitha Pindar Shaw who was full-blooded Cherokee."

"Oh yes, I recognize her from the painting you have over the mantelpiece back home," Mandie said with a slight intake of breath. *The young woman had been beautiful*, she thought, and Mandie wished she could have known her. She looked up at Uncle John, who was watching her and waiting with other photographs in his hands. "And she was your mother and my father's mother," she said.

"Yes," Uncle John replied as he handed her another photograph. "And this is her brother, Uncle Wirt, that you go to visit sometimes."

"Oh yes, Uncle Wirt when he must have been awfully young," Mandie said as she took the picture and looked at it.

John Shaw knew all the people in the photographs and explained each one to Mandie.

Before they knew it, Mrs. Taft appeared in the

doorway. "I hope y'all are at a stopping point," she said. "The food is on the table, and Ben has stabled your horse and buggy for the night."

John Shaw stood up, smiled, and said, "Thank you. I do feel a little hungry now."

Mandie knew the servants had not needed long to get dinner ready. The noon meal for Sunday was always cooked on Saturday and then warmed and put on the table after church. When they were finished eating, a large white tablecloth would be spread over the food on the table and left there for the evening meal. That allowed the servants to have most of the day off in observance of the Lord's Day.

Mandie quickly returned all the documents to the metal box and left it in the parlor while they went to eat. At the table, she explained to her grandmother about the will and her father's property.

"So you see, it's all mine now. All that has to be done is take the papers to the courthouse, and Uncle John is going to do that for me," Mandie said between bites of buttered squash.

Mrs. Taft looked at John Shaw and said with a big sigh, "Oh dear, what is going to happen to this child when she inherits everything we all own? I'm just afraid she's going to be weighted down with all that responsibility."

"I've thought about that, too," John Shaw said as he sliced the piece of ham on his plate. "Maybe some of us will live long enough to see Amanda grown up and old enough to handle these affairs herself."

"And maybe she'll end up with a husband who knows something about business," Mrs. Taft added.

Mandie gasped as she glanced from her grandmother to her uncle John. "Y'all sound like everybody is going to die and leave me alone," she said. "Let's don't talk about it. I don't want to talk about it." She felt a shiver go through her body at the very thought of losing any of her dear ones.

"We won't talk about it, but you do need to know that my lawyer is already taking care of what you will inherit from your father when you become of age," Uncle John told her.

"Inherit from my father? But that paper in that box gave me his property. What do I need with a lawyer?" Mandie asked.

"That property at Charley Gap is a very small amount of what will be coming to you," her uncle explained. "You see, when my father died—he was also your father's father—he left everything to your father and me, to be divided equally. Your father refused to accept anything when he went off to Swain County by himself; so his part is waiting for you to come of age. And when that time comes you will be very, very wealthy, I must say."

Mandie frowned and said, "But if my father didn't want it, maybe I don't want it either."

Uncle John looked at her and said, "Whether you want it or not, it will all be there for you when you are old enough."

"And of course you will inherit from me, Amanda," Mrs. Taft told her. "Part of my holdings are already in trust for you. The other part will go to your mother, but then since she doesn't have any other children her part will eventually go to you."

Mandie quickly laid down her fork on her plate, causing the china to ring with a low hum. "I don't want all this stuff you're talking about," she said, upset with the conversation. "I only want my mother, you, Uncle John, and you, Grandmother. I don't want what y'all *have*."

"But what we have has to be left to someone, Amanda, and of course that someone will be you," Uncle John said.

"I only want my father's house at Charley Gap, and you said it's mine now," Mandie told him.

"That's right," John Shaw agreed.

At that moment Ella, the downstair's maid, came to the doorway of the dining room. "Miz Taft, dat li'l friend of Missy 'Manda's from de school be at de door askin' for her."

"Celia?" Mandie quickly asked. "Is it Celia?"

"It sho' is," the maid replied.

"Ask her to come on in here, then, Ella," Mrs. Taft told her.

In a moment, Celia Hamilton appeared in the doorway. "Mrs. Taft, I got permission from Miss Prudence to spend the night here with Mandie if it's all right with you," Celia said.

"Of course, Celia, anytime," Mrs. Taft replied. "Come on in. Take off your cloak and sit down."

"Uncle Cal is waiting to see if I'm going to stay. I have to run back and let him know and get my bag out of the rig," Celia said, quickly disappearing down the hallway.

"I'm glad Celia is going to stay," Mandie was saying as her friend returned to the dining room and sat down next to Mandie at the table. She turned quickly to Celia and said, "Just wait 'til you hear what all happened at Joe Woodard's house while I was there."

"Oh dear!" Mrs. Taft suddenly exclaimed as she looked at the girls. "What have I done? Celia, Amanda has been exposed to the measles, and you shouldn't be here. I just didn't think."

"Oh, but, Mrs. Taft, I had the measles long years ago," Celia said with a smile.

"I do hope it's true that once you've had the measles you can't get it again," Mrs. Taft said with a big sigh.

"I've been around other people who have had the measles since I had them, and I didn't catch it again," Celia assured her.

John Shaw spoke up, "Dr. Woodward has always said you only get the stuff once."

"I do hope he's right," Mrs. Taft said.

The girls were eager to talk, and as soon as the meal was over, they went to the sun parlor to catch up on the latest happenings.

Chapter 3 / Thoughts About the Future

Before Celia even had a chance to sit down in the sun parlor, Mandie grabbed her hand and danced around the room, crying, "I have my father's house now. It's all my own! I own it! I own it!"

Celia looked at her in surprise and pulled her to a stop. "Oh, Mandie, that's wonderful! How did you get it?"

Mandie caught her breath and explained, "My father gave it to me. Joe and I found his will. It says he left it to me. It's *mine* now." She let go of Celia's hand, twirled around the room, and flopped onto the settee.

"Your father had a will? Where did you and Joe find it?" Celia asked as she sat down beside Mandie.

"It was in a metal box under the floor of his house," Mandie replied. She told her friend how she and Joe had broken in to the house because it was on fire and how they had found Irene sick inside.

"So your grandmother meant that you had been exposed to the measles because you were around Irene," Celia said.

"Yes, and Irene was awfully sick. I sure hope she gets well," Mandie said. "I know bad things happened, but if they hadn't I wouldn't have ever found the metal box."

Celia looked at Mandie with a big smile and said, "So now you don't have to promise any longer to marry Joe when y'all grow up—so he can get back your father's house for you."

Mandie frowned and fidgeted with her skirt as she replied, "No, and I told him that, and he got awfully mad at me. I would have to really love anyone I marry, whether it's Joe or someone else. And I think it would be a long, long time in the future before I would ever agree to marry anyone."

"Me, too," Celia said.

Mandie quickly changed the subject. "What are those men doing at the schoolhouse, putting in those electric lights and that furnace? Annie said they were making holes all over the place."

Celia gasped, clasped her hands together and said, "Oh yes, I'm scared nearly to death to stay in our room by myself. There's a big hole in the floor and another one in the wall. They are making a mess."

Mandie quickly looked at her friend and said with a big smile, "I have an idea. Maybe we could persuade Grandmother to let you stay here this week. You see, she told me I would have to stay out of school for a few days to be sure I was not coming down with the measles; so I can't go to school. You could go back and get your books and mine too.

And we could study here until Grandmother allows me to go back to school."

"Oh, that's a *great* idea!" Celia agreed excitedly. "But do you think Miss Prudence would allow me to do that? You have an excuse to stay out of school, but I don't."

"Grandmother could probably persuade Miss Prudence to agree. The only thing is, we'll have to persuade Grandmother to let us do that," Mandie said.

"And that might be hard to do," Celia added.

Mandie quickly stood up as she said, "Let's go in the parlor. Grandmother and Uncle John are probably in there." She started toward the door.

Celia got up and followed. "You do the talking, Mandie," she said.

"All right, leave it to me," Mandie replied as they went out into the hall and on down to the parlor.

Mrs. Taft and Uncle John were sitting by the fireplace, talking, but when Mandie and Celia came through the doorway, they instantly stopped their discussion. Mandie wondered what they had been talking about. Evidently they didn't want her and Celia to hear whatever they were saying. She and Celia sat down on a couple of stools near the fire.

"Well, did y'all get caught up on all the happenings since you last saw each other?" Mrs. Taft asked with a smile.

"Almost," Mandie replied as she looked at her grandmother and then at Uncle John, trying to decide how to broach the subject of school.

"Now, that sounds like you have something left over to talk about," Uncle John said with a teasing grin as he looked from Mandie to Celia.

Mandie shrugged her shoulders and said,

"You're right. I might as well tell you what it is." She paused again to look at her grandmother. "We were wondering if Celia could stay here this week with me while I have to stay out of school. We could study together. You see, she's all alone in our room, and there are holes in the floor and the wall, and she's scared by herself. Please."

Mrs. Taft and Uncle John exchanged looks.

"Well," Mrs. Taft began. Then she looked at Uncle John again and said to him, "You are her stepfather and the proper one to make the decision, I believe."

"Oh, but it's your house, Mrs. Taft," Uncle John said quickly.

"And since Uncle John is going home in the morning, Grandmother, you would be the one to have to ask Miss Prudence's permission," Mandie said.

Mrs. Taft was silent for a moment, cleared her throat, and said, "I suppose it would be all right, provided you girls really study."

"We will, Mrs. Taft," Celia finally spoke.

"I promise we will, Grandmother," Mandie said.

Mrs. Taft looked at Uncle John and asked, "Do you think Celia's mother would approve of this? We certainly couldn't get word to her fast enough to get permission."

"I think so," Uncle John said. "After all, we are all good friends."

Mrs. Taft thought for a moment and then said, "All right, then. I'll go over to the school in the morning to speak to Miss Prudence."

"I'll have to go with you to get my books—and Mandie's," Celia said. "And I may need more clothes if I'm going to stay all week."

"We'll go right after breakfast tomorrow," Mrs. Taft told her.

"Thank you, Mrs. Taft," Celia said.

"Yes, and I thank you, too, Grandmother," Mandie said. "Maybe it won't be so boring around here this week, after all. I'll have someone to do my lessons with!" Mandie smiled at her grandmother and said, "When will I be able to go back to school?"

"Probably in a few days," Mrs. Taft said. Then, looking at Uncle John, she asked, "Do you have any idea how long we should wait to see if Amanda is going to come down with the measles?"

Uncle John replied, "I suppose by the end of this coming week things should be cleared up, one way or another. I'd say the girls could return to school a week from tomorrow."

"I sure hope so, because I am not going to get the measles," Mandie said with a big sigh. "And I'm missing out on all the fun watching the men put electricity and that furnace into the school."

"Is that the only reason you're in such a hurry to get back to school?" Uncle John asked.

"No, sir," Mandie answered with a big smile. "You see, it's about time for another one of Miss Prudence's socials, and the boys from Mr. Chadwick's School will be coming over."

"Among whom, I believe, there is a young fellow by the name of *Patton*," her uncle teased.

"Well, Tommy Patton does go to Mr. Chadwick's School," Mandie answered. She grinned at him and straightened her skirts.

"Amanda, I do hope you are learning something and not going to that school for just the social side of it," Mrs. Taft said.

"Oh yes, ma'am, Grandmother, I'm learning a

lot of things. The socials are just like rewards for studying real hard," Mandie said.

"And we do learn how to behave as ladies for the future," Celia added.

"And Miss Prudence and Miss Hope always watch us to see if we're doing everything properly—the way we sit, the way we hold our cups, and all that silly stuff," Mandie added with a big grin.

"You may think all that is silly now, but when you are grown you will look at it differently, I'm sure," Mrs. Taft told her.

"I'm sorry, Grandmother," Mandie apologized. "I shouldn't say it's silly. It's just that I've never been used to being around people like that until I went to live with Uncle John after my father died. But I suppose I will have to live that way in the future."

"Why, Amanda," Uncle John said with a big laugh. "You sound disappointed that you're living the way we've all been used to." He winked at her and then asked, teasingly, "Could it be that you're more Cherokee in your thinking?"

Mandie frowned as she looked at her uncle and answered, "Yes, that must be what it is. After all, my grandmother—who was your mother—was full-blooded Cherokee." Mandie gave him a big smile.

Uncle John grinned as he replied, "Yes, I'm one-half Cherokee, and I'm pleased to know that you are proud of your heritage. But now you are learning the ways of my father, who was a full-blooded white man, and he was your grandfather. And your Grandmother Taft here is also white."

Mandie leaned forward in her chair as she said, "Uncle John, please take time one day soon to tell me all about my ancestors, how my grandfather met my Cherokee grandmother and all that."

"I promise I will, Amanda," Uncle John said. "As soon as you come home for a break from school we'll have some time together."

Mandie looked at her grandmother, who had been listening to the conversation. To her great surprise, Mrs. Taft said with a slight smile, "And, Amanda, you might be interested in what your uncle John can tell you about your mother and your father, how they met."

Uncle John glanced quickly at Mrs. Taft.

"Oh yes, Uncle John, I never get tired of talking about my father," Mandie said.

"When you come home, you and I will talk about all this," her uncle promised. "And I'm sure your mother will add her story."

Celia spoke up. "I think it's so exciting to have a friend who is related to the Cherokee people. And I've been able to meet so many of them. Mandie, you should write a book about your life story and about your parents and grandparents. Someday you'll have grandchildren who will be interested in all this, you know."

With a big sigh Mandie said, "Oh, Celia, I'd have to get married and have children first in order to have grandchildren. And I don't know that I ever want to get married."

Before Celia could reply, Mrs. Taft said with a little laugh, "Amanda, I'm sure you'll get married some day, when you're old enough. Most all girls do. You're just not at the age yet to be interested in such things."

Mandie glanced at Celia under half-closed eyes and saw that her friend was smiling as she mouthed the name "Joe." Mandie quickly shook her head.

"Yes, you have plenty of time ahead of you before you take that important step in your life," Uncle John agreed. He grinned at her and added, "Just think how old I was when I married your mother."

"But that was unusual because my father married my mother first," Mandie told him as she thought about her dear father who had died the previous year.

Everyone was silent in the room, and Mandie quickly stood up and said, "Now I think Celia and I will go for a walk." She looked at her friend, who also rose. "Do you want to?"

"Oh yes, Mandie, I do," Celia quickly agreed.

"Amanda, please don't leave the yard. Remember you were exposed to the measles, and you must stay away from other people," Mrs. Taft reminded her.

"We'll walk around the house for a while, just to get some exercise," Mandie promised as she and Celia left the room.

Once outdoors, the girls sat on a bench under a huge magnolia tree in the front yard. Even in the shade, the September afternoon was not cool enough for a wrap.

"Do you like living in so many different places, Mandie?" Celia asked.

"So many different places?" Mandie questioned. "Oh, you mean, here at Grandmother's, at the school, and back home—and sometimes at Uncle Ned's. Well, I suppose it's a lot of work, traveling from place to place. But it's always a change of scenery, so I don't get tired of it." She straightened her long skirts.

"I think I'd like it, too, but you know I only live at home or at school here," Celia told her as she pushed back her long curly auburn hair.

"But, Celia, you can always go with me wherever I go," Mandie said, quickly looking at her.

"Oh, but I couldn't, Mandie," Celia told her. "Whatever time I'm not at school here in Asheville I have to spend with my mother back in Richmond."

"Time seems to fly," Mandie said. "We are really getting older, aren't we?" She smiled at her friend.

"Naturally we're getting older, Mandie. We sure can't get any younger," Celia said with a giggle as she sat up straight and proper and adjusted her dress. "And I think I'll like being older."

"There are so many things we have to do before we're grown, but I suppose I'll be glad, too, when we get older, lots older," Mandie agreed.

Suddenly she remembered that she had news to tell Celia. "Joe told me this will probably be his last year at Mr. Tallant's school out there in Swain County, because he will have to go on to the university to learn to be a lawyer. And I suppose my mother most likely will want me to go on to the university, too, because I have to learn to take care of business."

"Oh, Mandie, that's wonderful, because my mother told me last week that she expects me to learn everything they can teach me here at school, and then she will enroll me in the university," Celia excitedly told her. "We'll be there together and with Joe, too."

"But, Celia, there are lots of universities. We may not go to the same one," Mandie said. "Besides, I would imagine Joe will still be two years ahead of us in school; so I'm not sure how that would work out."

Celia looked at her with a big smile and said,

"We can always ask to go to the same one he attends. And, who knows, maybe Robert Rogers will also go where we go."

"Celia, you really do like Robert, don't you?" Mandie said, smiling back. "You know I suggested to Joe that he could go to Mr. Chadwick's School here in Asheville where Robert goes, but he said Mr. Chadwick doesn't teach what he needs to learn to be a lawyer. I don't know what Robert wants to study, but he may not be planning to go wherever we go."

"I'll try to find out," Celia said, still smiling. "And if we don't go to the same university Joe goes to, maybe Robert and Tommy will attend the one we do."

Mandie thought about that for a moment and then laughed as she said, "Well, I sure hope Tommy and Robert, you and I, and Joe don't all end up together somewhere at the same school. That would never do."

"It might be interesting to create a little jealousy between Joe and Tommy," Celia teased.

"Oh, Celia, that's nonsense," Mandie said quickly.

"Mandie, I know Joe wants to marry you when you both grow up, but I also know Tommy is more than a little bit interested in you too," Celia replied as she tossed her long hair back.

"Celia, I look on both of them as just good friends of mine right now, and I'm sure anyone can have two good friends at one time," Mandie told her.

"But who knows what the future will bring?" Celia teased. "We'll probably be at least two years older when we leave here. We'll be fifteen years old; can you believe that?"

"Yes, and a lot of things can happen in the meantime," Mandie reminded her. "So let's don't plan too far ahead."

Mandie was secretly wondering how things would turn out for herself in the next two years. And she was sure she didn't want anything more than friendship from the two boys right now. She would have lots of time to think about love before then.

Chapter 4 / A Bad-Luck Day

The next morning Mandie anxiously awaited the return of her grandmother and Celia from the school. She was pretty sure Miss Prudence, the headmistress, would allow Celia to spend a few days at Mrs. Taft's house. Mrs. Taft had bought the schoolhouse building, which was a large, old-fashioned white clapboard house set on a hill amid magnificent magnolia trees. Mandie knew that the schoolmistress and her sister, Miss Hope, were grateful that the sale of the building had enabled them to keep open Misses Heathwood's School for Girls. And the two ladies were usually agreeable to any favors asked by Mrs. Taft.

"Come on, Snowball, let's go outside," Mandie told her white cat as she fastened on his red collar and leash. "We'll wait for Grandmother and Celia out there."

Snowball meowed in response. He looked up at his mistress and started to pull her toward the front door as she held the end of the leash. He had worn it enough to know that when Mandie put it on him they were going somewhere.

"Don't get in such a big hurry. I'm coming," Mandie told him as she tightened her hold on the leash and opened the front door. "Now, no shenanigans. Behave or I'll put you back inside." She closed the door behind them and walked across the porch to the steps.

Mandie paused to look out over the huge front yard. There was no sign of anyone on the road. She stepped down onto the walkway and went to sit on a bench at the edge of the grass, which was turning brown for the winter. Snowball hopped up beside her and sat looking around, evidently hoping for a bird or a squirrel to show up nearby.

Uncle John had left early that morning and had taken the metal box Mandie and Joe Woodard had found in her father's old house. He promised to take her father's will to the Swain County Courthouse as soon as he could get time. And if he found anything important in the other papers in the box, he would let her know.

Mandie had left the letters from her grandmother to her father in the bottom of the container. She didn't want to keep them with her because she didn't want to read the correspondence. She knew the whole story—about how her grandmother had separated her mother and her father by telling falsehoods, and how her grandmother now regretted this and had been anxious for Mandie to forgive her.

As she sat there alone, thinking about all this, she suddenly realized it was better to forgive and forget. "That's what I'm trying to do, forgive and forget," Mandie muttered aloud to herself. "And I believe my grandmother knows it."

Mandie kept her gaze on the road and her hand tightly holding the end of Snowball's red leash. She realized her grandmother had become a very important person in her life—a person Mandie loved and who loved her back and a supporter in most of the unusual activities Mandie found herself involved in whenever she tried to solve a mystery. She drew a deep breath as she wondered what she would ever have done without her grandmother nearby.

And at that moment she saw her grandmother's buggy approaching from down the road. She quickly stood up, tightened her hold on Snowball's leash, and walked over to the driveway, where her grandmother brought the buggy to a stop.

Mandie glanced at the baggage in the back as she quickly approached the vehicle. Celia was stepping down, and Mandie's grandmother was tossing the reins to Celia to loop over the hitching post.

"You're going to stay!" Mandie greeted her friend with a big smile.

"Yes, but only because I've been here with you, and you might be coming down with the measles," Celia said with a big laugh. "Miss Prudence says she is afraid I might carry the germ after I've been around you."

Mrs. Taft came around the vehicle to where Celia's bags were loaded. She said, "Let's get these things into the house. I think the three of us can manage without Annie's help."

Holding Snowball's leash, Mandie helped unload the buggy, and they carried Celia's clothes and the girls' books into the front hallway.

Annie, the maid, came to see who was coming

in the front door. "I he'p you, Missy," she told Celia as she took the armful of clothes the girl was carrying. Mandie quickly removed Snowball's leash and turned him free.

"And then, Annie, will you please get Ben to put up the horse and buggy?" Mrs. Taft told the maid who was going up the stairs. Glancing back at Mandie and Celia, she added, "Now you two girls get busy with your studies. You may use the back parlor for that this week." She followed Annie up the steps.

"Yes, ma'am," both the girls replied. They carried their books and walked down the hallway.

"You're only getting to stay here because I was exposed to the measles?" Mandie asked as they entered the back parlor and dumped their books onto the library table there.

"Well, you know how Miss Prudence is. She never really wants to let other people think she is giving in to their wishes," Celia said with a smile. "So when your grandmother told her about you and the measles, she agreed for me to stay here and study with you. However, she also told your grandmother she would expect us back to school by Friday if the measles didn't show up."

Mandie looked at her as they sat on the settee and asked, "By Friday? Miss Prudence thinks the scare of the measles will be gone by then."

"Yes, and your grandmother agreed," Celia said.

"I've been saying all the time I'm not going to get the measles," Mandie said with a big sigh.

Celia looked at her friend with a big smile and said, "Miss Prudence is having a social on Saturday, and the boys from Mr. Chadwick's School are coming over."

Mandie sat up straight and smiled back. "Then we'll get to see Tommy and Robert."

"That's right," Celia said, still smiling. "It sure was nice of Miss Prudence to request that we be back by Friday, wasn't it?"

"You mean you think Miss Prudence set that deadline so we would have to be back to school in time for the social?" Mandie asked.

Celia shrugged and said, "Well, Miss Prudence has her own reasons, I suppose, like having enough girls present to entertain the boys."

"Of course," Mandie agreed. "There are more students in Mr. Chadwick's School than we have. So Miss Prudence would be two girls short, which would leave a lot of boys on their own."

"And don't forget, Miss Prudence has these socials so we can learn to take our places in society when we grow up," Celia said with a mischievous grin.

Mandie shrugged and said, "We don't have to worry about that. By the time we grow up, society probably won't be so formal, and we'll manage." She looked at Celia and asked, "What are the workmen doing?"

"You ought to see the mess those men are making in the school," Celia replied. "They've made holes everywhere. I don't know how they'll ever be able to close them all up. I know they have to run pipes and wires through the floors, the walls, and the ceilings in the whole building in order to get the heat and electricity into each room, but it looks to me like they're going to have an awfully big job repairing all those holes."

"Do they have the heat or any of the lights working yet?" Mandie asked.

"Oh no. You see, they have to put a big furnace in the basement and connect all the rooms to that, and they couldn't heat up any place until the whole thing is done. And it's also the same with the lights. The wires all have to be connected outside to a pole," Celia explained.

"Well, I hope they get everything straightened up when they're finished," Mandie said. "And I want to get back to school so I'll have a chance to watch what they're doing." She stood up. "But right now I suppose we'd better do some studying." She went over to the table and picked up her notebook.

"Yes," Celia agreed as she followed her. She opened her notebook and took out a sheet of paper. "Miss Prudence wrote these instructions for us." She held the paper out to Mandie.

Mandie took it and scanned it. "We have to make a book report?" she questioned. "On what?" She looked at Celia.

"She said she didn't have time to talk with our teachers about everything, but that we should just read something out of your grandmother's library and write a report on it," Celia explained.

"That's easy homework," Mandie said with a smile. "I never have time to read much. Let's go look over Grandmother's books."

The girls went to the library down the hall and browsed through the book-lined walls. Finally making their selections, they returned to the back parlor. Mandie curled up in a big chair by the window, and Celia sat on the settee. They were both so absorbed in their books that they were surprised when

Ella, the downstairs maid, came in and said, "Time to eat."

Mandie and Celia looked up at her.

"Eat?" Mandie said, reaching for a piece of paper from her notebook to mark her place in the book she was reading.

"I suppose it is time for the noon meal," Celia said as she closed her book after inserting a scrap of paper.

"Now, don't be tellin' me you girls are not hungry," Ella teased as she turned to go back down the hallway.

The girls followed. When they were seated at the table, Mandie suddenly realized she had a headache and rubbed her forehead with her hand.

Mrs. Taft saw her and quickly asked, "What's wrong, dear?" She passed the corn to Celia.

"Oh, nothing. I have a little headache from reading, I suppose," Mandie said with a smile as she reached for a biscuit from the platter in front of her.

Celia spoke up, "So do I. And it's going to take time to read those books we picked out."

Mrs. Taft silently looked from one girl to the other and frowned.

Mandie noticed and explained, "Miss Prudence gave us an assignment to read a book out of your library and make a report on it, which we have to do and have ready by the time we go back to school Friday."

She took a sip of water from her glass and was suddenly alarmed when she realized her throat seemed to be sore. She began wondering how the measles start. *Could I be coming down with something?* she asked silently. *The measles? No, no, no,* she told herself. *I am not going to get the measles.*

"Yes, I promised Miss Prudence I would bring you girls back to school first thing Friday morning," Mrs. Taft said as she began eating. "So y'all be sure you have your homework done."

As Mandie put a forkful of mashed potatoes in her mouth, she was barely able to keep a straight face as the food burned her throat when she swallowed. She frowned and thought, *Too much pepper. That's what's wrong.* She left the potatoes on her plate and buttered her biscuit. She bit into it and, as she swallowed, she thought, *That feels better but not quite right.*

"My mother came to visit me at school last week, and she said we might go to New York when we have a school break—" Celia said.

Mandie interrupted, "New York?" She looked at her grandmother and asked, "Oh, Grandmother, could we go to New York, too? We could go visit Jonathan Guyer and—"

Mrs. Taft interrupted her, saying, "Amanda, we are not going to New York. We have no reason to visit the Guyers." She laid down her fork and frowned.

"But you know Mr. Guyer from way back, and we had such fun with Jonathan on our journey to Europe," Mandie protested.

"That's enough about New York," Mrs. Taft said firmly. "Now you girls finish your food." She picked up her cup and drank her coffee.

Mandie didn't understand why her grandmother was so stern about not going to New York. She frowned and glanced at Celia, who also looked puzzled.

When the meal was over, Mandie hoped her grandmother would not notice that she had not eaten very much. But it seemed that the mention of New York had distracted her grandmother. Mrs. Taft rose from the table and said, "You girls get back to your lessons. I will see y'all at suppertime." She hurriedly left the room as the girls slowly followed.

As soon as they were once again in the back parlor, Mandie drew a deep sigh and said, "For some reason Grandmother doesn't want to talk about New York. I wonder why." She picked up her book and flopped into the chair.

Celia sat down on the settee as she prepared to resume her reading.

"I don't know, Mandie," Celia said. "Maybe something else is bothering your grandmother."

"Tell me, Celia," Mandie said. "If you and your mother do go to New York, are y'all going to visit Jonathan?"

"Jonathan? I had not even thought about seeing him and, since my mother doesn't know him or his family, I doubt that we would visit him," Celia replied.

"But, Celia, remember when we said goodbye we promised we would visit him if we went to New York, and he said maybe he could come down here to see us, too," Mandie reminded her. "Oh, I wish I could go with y'all."

"Mandie, I'm not sure we are even going to New York," Celia said. "My mother only said we *might* go."

"I hope you do get to go," Mandie told her. "And if you do I hope my grandmother will at least give me permission to go with you and your mother if Grandmother doesn't want to go."

"Oh, that would be wonderful, Mandie," Celia

said with a smile. "I'm sure my mother would like for you to go."

"When do you think you'll go?" Mandie asked as she opened her book.

"I have no idea, Mandie," Celia replied. "We won't have a school break until Thanksgiving week, and then the next one would be at Christmas, I suppose."

Mandie thought for a moment, and then she said, "Celia, I don't think I could go at Christmas because I'd like to be home with my mother then. Maybe you could make it Thanksgiving."

"Maybe your mother could go with us," Celia suggested.

"No," Mandie said, shaking her head. "It's going to take a long time for her to get over that terrible fever she had this summer. I don't think she'll be traveling anywhere this winter."

"Then I'll see if I can talk my mother into going to New York during Thanksgiving week," Celia decided.

"If my grandmother doesn't agree for me to go without my mother's permission, I'll just write and ask my mother when you know for sure you're going," Mandie replied.

"I'll let you know when," Celia promised.

The girls returned to their reading. Mandie had a little nagging fear about the measles as her throat became more irritated and her headache worse. There was definitely something wrong. And as the afternoon passed, she felt worse and worse. Maybe if she quit thinking about it, it would go away. She was determined it was not going to be the measles.

Mandie tried to concentrate on her book, but she kept glancing at Celia, who was completely absorbed in her own reading. She heard the grand-father clock in the hallway strike three, and she stood up to stretch.

"I'm tired of sitting," she said to Celia as her friend looked up at her.

Celia smiled and laid her book down. "Me, too," she said as she rose from the settee.

"Want to walk outside for a little while?" Mandie asked.

"Let's do," Celia agreed.

As the girls started toward the doorway, Snow-ball came running into the parlor. Mandie stooped down and picked up the white cat.

"I suppose you want to go, too," she said to the cat. "Let me get your leash."

The girls stopped at the hall tree in the front hall-way so Mandie could get Snowball's leash from one of the hooks and put it on him.

"You don't trust him to stay in the yard?" Celia asked as she watched Mandie buckle the red leash.

Mandie straightened up and held the end of the leash. "I don't want him running off because Grand-mother said I couldn't go out of the yard," she ex-plained.

"Good idea. I know how much Snowball likes to run away," Celia agreed.

The girls went outside and walked around the yard. Mandie kept a hold on Snowball's leash. The September day was warm and sunny, but Mandie felt cold. A shiver ran over her, and she wished she had put on a jacket.

"Are you cold, Mandie?" Celia asked.

"Well, aren't you? Seems a little cool out here to me," Mandie said, nervously walking about.

"No, not exactly," Celia said, still watching her.

"Maybe we ought to go back inside, if you're cold."

"All right, I suppose we should keep on with our books or we'll never get them read in time to write reports," Mandie agreed.

They went back to the parlor and continued their reading. Snowball curled up on the settee next to Celia and went to sleep.

At the supper table that night, Mandie felt so terrible she couldn't eat. She kept pushing food around on her plate and had nothing to say.

"Are you not hungry, Amanda?" her grandmother asked.

Mandie looked across at her without answering.

"Amanda, are you not feeling well?" Mrs. Taft asked as she watched Mandie.

Mandie felt tears come into her eyes for no reason and couldn't answer. She dropped her gaze and shook her head.

"Oh, dear, why didn't you tell me you're not feeling well?" Mrs. Taft asked as she instantly stood up and came around the table to Mandie's side. "Let's get you into bed."

Mandie was still not able to speak without bursting into tears, so she stood up and allowed her grandmother to lead her to her room. Celia followed. Annie, the maid, was in the hallway, and Mrs. Taft spoke to her.

"Let's get her in bed, and then ask Ben to come see me," Mrs. Taft said. "Dr. Woodard is due in town tomorrow morning to see Mrs. Edwards, and I want Ben to take a message over there for me."

Mandie heard everything but did not reply. She didn't protest when Annie and Mrs. Taft helped her undress and get into bed. Then Annie left to find Ben.

"Everything is going to be all right, dear," Mrs. Taft told her as she pulled up the covers. "I'll be right back." She turned to look at Celia, who had stayed in the room. "Dear, would you please just sit here until I get back?"

"Of course, Mrs. Taft, anything I can do to help," Celia replied as she sat in the big chair near the bed.

Mandie lay there with her eyes closed, silently worried. *It couldn't be the measles,* she thought. *She was sure she was not going to get the measles.* Celia moved over to sit on the side of the bed as she grasped Mandie's hand and squeezed it. Mandie returned the squeeze without moving.

Mrs. Taft was back in a few minutes. "Ben has gone to the Edwardses' to leave the message for Dr. Woodard," she told Mandie as she bent over her and straightened the covers. "Now you just rest and try to get some sleep. I'll be right here."

Mandie slightly nodded her head in reply but didn't open her eyes.

"I can stay here with her, Mrs. Taft," Celia offered.

"No, dear, I was going to suggest you get your things and move into the next room for the night," Mrs. Taft said softly. "Annie will help me. Thank you, dear, and if we need you, we'll call you."

Mandie heard Annie come back into the room and felt the maid place a hot water bottle at her feet. The warmth felt so good. She heard Annie helping Celia move into the adjoining room as she drifted off to sleep.

During the night, Mandie dreamed that she was arguing with Dr. Woodard. She told him she did not have the measles and was not going to get them, but he seemed sure she had the measles.

Chapter 5 / Under the Weather

The next morning Mandie could hear someone calling her name. She managed to get her heavy eyelids open and looked straight into the face of Dr. Woodard, who was sitting next to the bed and holding her hand.

"Ah, Miss Amanda, I knew you were playing 'possum with me," the old doctor said as he smiled at her.

Mandie looked around the room. Celia was standing in front of the fireplace where a fire blazed away. Mandie frowned as she remembered the night before when her grandmother had put her to bed. Trying to speak, she realized her throat was awfully sore, and her voice cracked as she asked in alarm, "Dr. Woodard, I don't have the measles, do I?"

Dr. Woodard squeezed her hand and smiled as he replied, "I don't think so. What you've got is an awfully bad cold."

At that instant Mandie sneezed and pushed herself back against her pillow. "I've been telling everybody I'm not going to get the measles," she said. Looking into the old man's kind face, she added, "But I'm awfully tired."

"Young lady, that's because you've been running around the country so much—that long journey to Europe and then to Uncle Ned's house and then to my house. I'm ordering lots of rest so you'll be ready to return to school on Friday, which is the day your grandmother said you and Miss Celia would be going back."

"Yes, sir," Mandie said, lowering her voice to a whisper as she looked at him. Then she remembered how sick her stepsister had been. "Dr. Woodard, is Irene all right?"

Dr. Woodard paused before he replied, "Well, not all right, but on the way there if she takes care of herself. The measles can be a terrible sickness."

"Joe? Is he all right?" Mandie asked as her voice cracked again with a hoarse cough. Her heart beat wildly as she waited for his answer.

"Joe's fine. I don't believe he will get the measles, but we lost the little Guyton girl," he said sadly, rubbing his forehead with his handkerchief.

Tears came into Mandie's eyes. She had not known the girl, but Gretchen had been in Joe's school, and Dr. Woodard had been to see her while Mandie was visiting the Woodards. Gretchen Guyton had died from the measles.

At that moment Mrs. Taft came into the room and, when she saw that Mandie was awake, she rushed to the bed. "Dear, I'm so glad to see you're awake," she said as she brushed Mandie's blond hair back from her face.

Mandie's blue eyes filled with tears as she

reached for her grandmother's hand. "I don't have the measles, Grandmother," she said in a hoarse voice.

"That's what Dr. Woodard told me," Mrs. Taft said with a big smile. "Now all we have to do is get rid of this cold you have."

Mandie looked at Celia over by the fireplace and asked, "Celia, what time is it? I can't see the clock from here." She rubbed her eyes.

"Why, it's ten minutes after eight, Mandie," Celia told her as she looked at the clock on the mantel. "Mandie, I'm so glad you're better."

"Thank you, Celia," Mandie said as she tried to sit up, but she got tangled in the bedcovers.

Dr. Woodard stood up and moved his chair away from the bed.

Mrs. Taft bent to help straighten out the covers and then plumped up the pillows as Mandie sat up.

"Do you think you could eat something? A little broth maybe?" her grandmother asked.

"That's just what you need right now, Miss Amanda," Dr. Woodard told her. "You've got to regain your strength."

Mandie smiled up at him and asked, "Couldn't I have grits instead and maybe a buttered biscuit?" Her voice was still husky.

"You certainly may," the old man said, smiling back. "Anything you want."

"Well, I'm hungry, even if I can't talk very well this morning," Mandie explained, her voice cracking. "That's why I asked Celia what time it is. I wanted to know if I'd missed breakfast."

Mrs. Taft stooped to squeeze Mandie's hand. "I'm so glad," she said. "Half the battle against the cold is won if you can eat."

Mandie looked up at her and said, "But I don't think I want to go downstairs to eat—"

Mrs. Taft interrupted, "Of course not, dear. I wouldn't allow that anyway. I'll get Annie to bring up a tray."

"I'll go tell her, Mrs. Taft," Celia offered.

"Thank you, dear," Mrs. Taft replied.

"And bring up the books that we were reading, Celia," Mandie told her friend.

Celia paused to look back at Mandie and asked, "The books? Do you think you ought to read?"

"I have to do something. I can't just stay here in bed," Mandie replied.

Celia looked at Dr. Woodard and Mrs. Taft.

"Miss Celia, go ahead and bring your books. I don't think Miss Amanda will overdo the reading," Dr. Woodard said as he smiled at Mandie. "I'm going to give her a tonic that will make her too sleepy to read much."

"Yes, sir," Celia said as she left the room.

Mandie quickly looked at Dr. Woodard and said, "I don't want to sleep all the time."

Dr. Woodard walked back toward the bed and said, "Now, Miss Amanda, I told you I was going to recommend lots of rest, and, knowing you, the only way that can be achieved is to slow you down a little. In a few days you'll be as good as new."

"Yes, Amanda, you have to do what the doctor says," Mrs. Taft said. "Otherwise your cold could get worse and it could be dragged out longer."

Mandie sighed loudly and said, "Well, right now I'm too tired to fuss about it."

Mrs. Taft looked at Dr. Woodard over Mandie's head.

Dr. Woodard caught her glance and said to Mandie with a little laugh, "That's good that you're too tired to fuss. You won't wear yourself out fussing, then."

Mandie smiled back at him and said with a hoarse voice, "Just give me time. How long are you going to be here, Dr. Woodard?"

"I'll be around for two or three days probably. I have several other patients in this area that I need to see," he told her.

"And he'll be staying here with us," Mrs. Taft added.

Celia returned with their books. Dr. Woodard said, "Miss Celia, I don't think you ought to have contact with Miss Amanda, or you might catch her cold."

Celia paused on her way to Mandie's bed and looked at him.

"You'll probably be all right if you just stay over there on the other side of the room by the fire," the old man explained. "You can keep Miss Amanda company that way."

"And you'll also be a great help to me," Mrs. Taft told the girl. "You will be able to let me know if Amanda needs anything."

"Celia, you've got to stay so I'll have someone to talk to," Mandie added.

"All right," Celia agreed as she handed Mandie's book to Mrs. Taft, who in turn laid it on Mandie's bedside table. "I had planned on staying with you. After all, I got excused from school this week in order to stay here." She walked back over to the fireplace and sat in a big chair nearby.

"Thank you, Celia," Mandie said in a whisper-voice.

Just then, Annie came in with the tray of food.

Mrs. Taft helped Mandie plump up her pillows again so she could sit up in the bed.

"I'm cold," Mandie said as Annie set the tray on the table by the bed and left the room.

"I'll get something to go around your shoulders," Mrs. Taft said. She hurried to the tall wardrobe, took down a warm robe, and brought it back to drape around Mandie.

"Thank you, Grandmother. That feels better," Mandie said as she looked at the tray. "If you would set the tray by me here on the bed, I think I could manage better."

Mrs. Taft smoothed a place in the covers and set the tray on the bed. "Now if you can handle this all right, I think Dr. Woodard and I will go downstairs for a cup of coffee while you eat. We've already had breakfast, but I could use another cup of coffee, couldn't you, Dr. Woodard?" she asked as she looked at him.

"I certainly could," Dr. Woodard agreed and, looking back at Mandie as he followed Mrs. Taft out the door, he added, "I'll be back to give you your tonic after you finish eating."

Mandie didn't reply. She just sighed as he and her grandmother left the room. Then, looking across the room at Celia, she said, "Thanks for staying, Celia. I'm sorry I got this silly cold and ruined our week away from school."

"I'm just glad it's a cold you got and not the measles," Celia replied as she curled up in the big chair.

"So am I," Mandie agreed as she poured a little of the coffee in the pot into her cup and sipped it. The liquid burned her throat and she set it down.

"Leave the lid off the pot and let it cool," Celia

suggested as she watched from across the room.

"Right," Mandie agreed as she removed the lid from the pot. She picked up the small glass of orange juice and sipped it. It didn't feel too good going down her sore throat but she managed to swallow some of it. "Oh, shucks!" she moaned as she set the glass back on the tray and slid down on the bed.

Celia looked across the room at Mandie's tray and asked, "Do you know of anything else I could get you to eat?"

"No, thank you, Celia," Mandie said with a hoarse voice.

"Not even the chocolate candy I brought back from the school yesterday?" Celia asked with a grin.

Mandie rolled her eyes and said, "This is the first time in my life I've ever refused candy, but I don't think I could swallow it."

"Oh, Mandie," Celia said with a gasp. "I'm sorry."

"That's all right. I'll eat it Friday when we go back to school," Mandie told her. She was too miserable to even think about returning to school. Maybe the tonic Dr. Woodard was going to give her would make her feel better.

But when she drank the nasty-tasting liquid, later she fell asleep. Every time she woke up after that, someone was poking a spoonful of the stuff at her to drink again. *Oh well*, she thought. *At least she wasn't wide awake and in misery.*

On Thursday morning she woke up feeling just fine. Her cold was gone. She went downstairs for breakfast with her grandmother and Celia, and ate as though she had been starved. She was happy to be feeling good again.

"I suppose you girls remember that President McKinley will be buried today," Mrs. Taft said, looking directly at Mandie.

Tears came into Mandie's blue eyes as she said, "I wish we could have gone."

"Yes, ma'am," Celia said in reply to Mrs. Taft.

"That would have been impossible, dear," Mrs. Taft explained. "You see, his body is at his and Mrs. McKinley's home this morning—for a private viewing. Then he will be taken to the Methodist church there in Canton, Ohio, for the service is to be held at two o'clock. The casket will be taken to the vault at West Lawn Cemetery afterwards. So you see, dear, it was more or less a family thing in the end."

"I know his wife loved him, but he belonged to us, too. He was our president," Mandie said. "So I just wish we could have been there."

"At least we're lucky that we have Vice-President Theodore Roosevelt for our president now," Celia said. "If President McKinley had been killed during his first term, after Vice-President Hobard died, we would have been without a president or a vice-president." Then, looking at Mandie, she said, "I brought our history books from school, and I've been reading about all our presidents while you've been sleeping this week."

"I'm wide awake now, so I suppose I'll have to get back to reading that book so I can write my book report for tomorrow," Mandie said. "And you've probably already done yours."

Celia smiled at her and said, "I've read the book, but I haven't written the report yet. In fact, I read the book you're supposed to be reading, too."

"You did?" Mandie replied with a big smile. "Then, if you would just tell me what it is about I wouldn't have to read it. I could just write my book report."

"Oh no," Celia replied quickly, grinning broadly. "I'm not doing your homework for you just because you got that silly cold."

Mrs. Taft looked at both girls and said, "Now if you all are finished with breakfast, I think you'd better get that book and get started, Amanda. I'm sure Celia can write her report and then find more studying to do." She rose from the table.

Mandie and Celia also stood up as they both chimed, "Yes, ma'am."

Then Mrs. Taft spoke again, "Now, Amanda, I don't want you to have a relapse. Just take your time and get the book read, and if you want to you may get back into bed and read it there."

Mandie looked at her grandmother in surprise. "In bed? No, Grandmother, I've been in the bed too much this week already. I'll be all right," she said, smiling at Mrs. Taft. Then she remembered the visit from Dr. Woodard. "Did Dr. Woodard go home?"

"Yes, dear. He left yesterday, but he's visiting patients on his way home," Mrs. Taft replied as they all started to leave the dining room. "And I know where to find him if we need him."

"But, Grandmother, we won't need him. I only had a little old cold," Mandie said. She had never seen her grandmother so concerned about her.

"I know, Amanda, but a cold can come back if you don't take care of yourself," Mrs. Taft said as they stepped into the hallway. "Now I'm going to be busy in the library with some correspondence. You girls go back to the little parlor and get that school-work done."

"Yes, ma'am," the two girls said as they continued down the corridor to the back parlor.

As they stood in the doorway, Mandie stopped and said with a laugh, "Look, Snowball is asleep on top of my book." She pointed to the table where the cat was curled up on the book. He heard them, unwound, stood up, and stretched.

"He was trying to do your homework for you," Celia said with a giggle.

Mandie reached to pat his head as he looked up at her and meowed. "Snowball, you'd better make haste to the kitchen if you want anything to eat."

Snowball blinked his blue eyes, meowed again, jumped down from the table, and ran out of the room.

"You see what a smart cat he is?" Mandie asked giggling. "He understood what I said."

Celia took her notebook from the table and sat in a chair as she prepared to write her book report. Mandie picked up her book, curled up on the settee, and propped on the pillows.

After a few silent minutes, Mandie stuck her finger into her book to hold her place and said, "I'm so anxious to get back to school I can't keep my mind on this book. I want to see what they're doing to get the electricity and furnace put in."

"And I want to get back so I can decide what I will wear to the social on Saturday," Celia told her as she stopped writing in her notebook.

"Oh, I hadn't even thought about that," Mandie replied. "But how are we going to have a social if the schoolhouse is all messed up with holes everywhere and workmen all over the place?"

"Don't worry," Celia told her. "Miss Prudence will see that her social is done properly. Maybe she'll even cover up the holes with satin ribbons around them or something silly like that. And I'm sure she won't let the men work during the time Mr. Chadwick's School is visiting us."

Mandie laughed as she said, "It would be really funny if one of those workmen popped up in the middle of our tea, just when Miss Prudence is watching to see that we hold our cups and saucers right."

"Or if they pounded away on pipes in the basement while we're supposed to be carrying on what she calls a 'proper conversation' with the boys," Celia added with a laugh. "She made an announcement last week that we would have a special guest, and we've all been wondering who that could be."

"A special guest?" Mandie repeated. "Maybe Grandmother knows who it is."

"No," Celia replied. "I asked Mrs. Taft about it while you were asleep yesterday, and she said we would just have to wait and see."

"You know my grandmother," Mandie said. "She usually knows everything that's going on, especially at the school. She probably does know, and is not telling."

"Anyhow, Robert Rogers will probably be there," Celia said with a big smile.

"And Thomas Patton," Mandie added. As she spoke she realized there couldn't be many more socials ahead because eventually they would all go on to higher education and to their separate ways.

Even after she went to bed that night, Mandie was still thinking about her future. She was growing up even though she wasn't sure she wanted to.

Chapter 6 / A Scary Situation

Early Friday morning, Mrs. Taft sent Mandie and Celia back to school in her rig. Her driver, Ben, who was always in a hurry, pulled up in the driveway at the front door of the school with a sudden jolt.

"Heah we be," Ben said as he jumped down to see about their bags.

Mandie and Celia stepped down from the rig. Mandie looked around as she said, "I don't see any workmen."

"Miss Prudence makes them stay in the back-yard. They're forbidden to use the front entrance," Celia explained as they walked up the steps to the long front porch and into the schoolhouse.

"I don't see any holes, Celia," Mandie said as she surveyed the hallway.

"Miss Prudence has them all hidden in here. She had the furniture put in front of them so you can't see them when you walk in," Celia replied. She pointed to one wall and said, "There are a couple holes behind that chest over there.''

Ben came in behind them and placed their bags at the bottom of the huge staircase going up to the second floor. ''Need me to carry dis heah stuff up de stairs?'' he asked.

''No thank you, Ben,'' Mandie told him. ''We can get it up to our room. Thanks for bringing us back to school.''

''Yessum,'' he said. ''Den I be on my way.'' He went back outside.

At that moment the dining room doors down the corridor opened, and students came out.

''Oh, that must be the second sitting. We'd better get our things up to the room and get ready for class,'' Mandie remarked.

Some of the girls greeted Mandie and Celia as they rushed by them up the staircase. Mandie looked up and saw Aunt Phoebe, the school housekeeper, coming down.

Mandie stepped over to meet her. ''Good morning, Aunt Phoebe,'' she greeted her. ''I finally got back.''

''So I sees,'' Aunt Phoebe replied as she put an arm around Mandie. ''And I'se so glad you made it back what with all dem measles where you been.'' She turned to embrace Celia as she added, ''And you didn't git dat stuff either, did you?''

''No, ma'am,'' Celia replied. ''I had the measles several years ago.''

The old woman picked up two of the valises. ''Come on, gotta git a movin'. We git dis heah stuff up to yo' room fo' dat bell ring to go to class,'' she told them as she turned to go back up the steps.

''Oh, thank you, Aunt Phoebe. We would have had to make two trips to get it all up there,'' Mandie said as she and Celia picked up their other bags.

"Where are all the holes, Aunt Phoebe?" Mandie asked as they ascended the staircase.

"Dey jes' ev'rywhere, and de workmen be causin' all dis heah dust and spiders and rats, and dey making all dat noise. Cain't heah myself think sometimes," the old woman explained.

"I don't hear any noise," Mandie said as they got to the hallway outside their room.

"Jes' you wait," Aunt Phoebe told her. "Miz Prudence, she don't 'llow no noise until aftuh de breakfus' done wid. Den dey started real good fo' de day."

Celia stepped ahead and pushed open the door to their room. Mandie followed and looked around as Aunt Phoebe deposited the valises she was carrying and rushed back out.

"I gotta git back to work now," the old woman said. "You girls hurry up now, and don't be late for class."

"Yes, ma'am," Mandie said. "Thanks for helping us."

"Yes, thank you, Aunt Phoebe," Celia added.

The old woman closed the door behind her as she left. Mandie walked around the room. Celia began pulling her notebook and school books out of her bag.

"Where are the holes?" Mandie asked.

"Oh, Mandie, there's one under our bed, and there's another one under that rug by the window. But right now you'd better get your books and get going," Celia said. She took off her coat and hung it up on a peg by the wardrobe.

Mandie quickly opened her bag and took out her books. "If we have time between classes, will you show me all these holes you said they were making?" she asked as she stood up and removed her cape to put it next to Celia's coat.

"I won't have to show you, Mandie, because you'll see holes everywhere we go, unless Miss Prudence has had them temporarily covered, but then the workmen have to uncover them in order to run pipes and wires through," Celia told her as they went out into the hallway and down the stairs to their first class of the day.

"How long do you think these workmen will be around?" Mandie asked as they came to the doorway of their literature classroom and stopped to talk.

"Miss Prudence is getting impatient with them, but the men tell her that it's impossible to do a job like this any faster than they're going," Celia replied. "And they told her they *might* be finished by Thanksgiving or at the latest by the Christmas holidays."

"So we have to live here with holes everywhere until they do get done. And there's nothing Miss Prudence can do about it, I suppose," Mandie said.

At that moment there was a loud clanging noise that sounded like someone banging on iron pipes. The two girls jumped and looked at each other, then laughed. Other students came along behind them, and they all entered the classroom. Miss Willoughby, their literature teacher, was already behind her desk at the front of the room. The bell in the backyard rang, and the girls quickly took their seats.

"Good morning, young ladies," Miss Willoughby greeted them in her British accent. This was her first year teaching in the United States, and sometimes Mandie had trouble understanding what she was saying.

The banging continued, and the teacher raised her voice even more as she told them, "I have been informed the workmen will be in this area of the school today. So it will be impossible to carry on any lecture. Therefore, I would like for you to pass up your book reports, and then get out your notebooks and write the report again from memory." There was a lull in the banging noise.

There was a faint murmur among the girls, and Miss Willoughby explained, "I am not having you repeat work. I am testing your memories. You should be able to retain most of the knowledge you acquire here in your studies."

The students passed their book reports to the front of the class, where the girl sitting nearest Miss Willoughby collected them and took them to the teacher.

"Thank you. Now please begin writing," Miss Willoughby instructed them as the noise boomed through the room again.

The girls wrote their reports from memory and handed them in at the end of the class period. Mandie breathed a sigh of relief as the noise ceased, and she and Celia went on to their next class.

Then it was the same thing all over again, loud noises interrupting all their other classes, ceasing only during the noon meal and finally ending at suppertime.

During the day, Mandie was able to see quite a few holes in the floors and walls. Celia already knew where they were and pointed them out to her. After supper that night, Miss Prudence asked everyone into the parlor and made an announcement.

"Young ladies," Miss Prudence began as she stood before the group seated in the parlor, "we will be having a very special person at our tea tomorrow—Miss Eva Marie Marston. She is well-known throughout the country as a pianist and singer, and she will play and sing tomorrow afternoon while Mr. Chadwick's students are here. Mrs. Taft, Amanda Shaw's grandmother, has arranged this for us." She paused.

Mandie glanced at Celia and thought, *My grandmother didn't tell me about this!* Then she became aware that the other girls were looking at her.

Miss Prudence continued, "And Mrs. Taft has suggested we make Miss Marston an offer to stay here the remainder of this school year so that any of you young ladies who are interested may have the opportunity of studying with her." She paused again and looked around the room.

Several of the students smiled and nodded. Then suddenly it dawned on Mandie that her grandmother was doing this because she wanted Mandie to have piano lessons or voice lessons—or both.

"Please be on your best behavior tomorrow, young ladies. Now you are dismissed," Miss Prudence finished and left the room.

The students stood up and moved about the parlor as they discussed the possibility of piano and voice lessons. Mandie listened, then turned to Celia and said, "My grandmother could have at least told me about this ahead of time." They stood by the fireplace where a fire warmed them.

"But, Mandie, that would be jumping ahead of Miss Prudence. After all, Miss Prudence is the one who runs this school," Celia replied.

"I know. But I'm sure my grandmother initiated

this visit by Miss Eva Marie Marston. And since my grandmother saved the school for Miss Prudence and Miss Hope by buying the building, Miss Prudence seems to think she has to let my grandmother make decisions on how to run the school," Mandie said.

At that precise moment, April Snow walked by Mandie and Celia and said, "So your grandmother *is* running the school now!" The tall girl turned and looked at Mandie with her deep black eyes as she pushed back her long black hair.

Mandie knew April was always trying to cause trouble, so she didn't reply. She didn't want to get into a conversation with her.

"So you don't want to talk about it," April added when she received no response from Mandie. Then she leaned forward, within inches of Mandie and said in an angry voice, "You'd better not get me involved in this music business, or you'll be sorry, I swear on my pirate ancestors' reputation."

Finally Mandie couldn't be silent anymore. "So you have pirate ancestors? So what? I have Cherokee ancestors!" she replied in a haughty voice.

"Pirates are smarter than your old Indians, any day," April answered as she spun around on her heels and walked across the room.

Mandie watched her leave. "She always seems to get the last word, but she'd better watch out. One day I might get even," she said with an angry frown.

"Why don't we go to our room and unpack our bags?" Celia asked as she watched April Snow walk down the hallway. April turned and gave them both a challenging glance. "Come on, Mandie," Celia said as she started toward their room.

"I suppose we do need to get our things hung

up," Mandie agreed as she followed Celia out into the hallway and up the staircase.

"And we have to read the next chapter in our history book, too."

Once inside their room, Mandie relaxed as she emptied out her bags, hung up her clothes, and put the rest of her things in the bureau drawers. Then she remembered the holes Celia had said were in the floor. Quickly getting down on her knees, she asked Celia, "Where is the hole under the bed?" She tried to see under the quilt hanging down on the side.

Celia came over and flopped down beside her. She raised the quilt and said, "Right there, under that little rug that I put over it. See?" She pulled the rug forward, exposing a large hole in the floor near the mopboard.

"Oh, goodness. That is a big hole," Mandie said in surprise as she peeked under the bed.

"Big enough for a rat to come out of," Celia said as she pulled the rug back over the hole. "That's why I covered them up like that," she said as she pointed to another rug in the room.

Mandie moved back on her heels and said, "And the other one over there, is it that large?" She got to her feet and went to pull the rug Celia had indicated covering another hole.

"You see, it's as big as the other one," Celia said. "I've been wondering if a rat could push the rug up and come on into our room." She looked at Mandie with a worried expression.

"I don't think so, not as long as they are covered with these heavy rugs. But I really don't know," Mandie replied as she spread the rug back over the hole near the window. "Maybe the workmen will get these closed up pretty soon."

"I'm not so sure it will be soon," Celia said as she sat in one of the big chairs by the fireplace and opened her history book.

Mandie took her history book and curled up in the other chair by the fireplace. She could feel the warmth of the fire, and it felt good. "You know, Celia, I'm not sure I want that furnace in this school-house, because we won't have a fire in the fireplace anymore to sit by," she said.

"I know everybody is saying we won't use the fireplaces anymore, but maybe we could once in a while," Celia replied.

"Maybe on special occasions," Mandie agreed. Then, looking at her friend, she asked, "What are you wearing to the social tomorrow afternoon?"

"I haven't made my mind up yet," Celia replied as she pulled her legs up under her long skirts. "I'm anxious to see and hear Miss Marston tomorrow. She was in Richmond one day this past summer, but my mother didn't have time to go to her concert, and Aunt Rebecca was out of town."

"Are you going to study with her if Miss Prudence persuades her to stay?" Mandie asked.

"I'd love to," Celia said with a big smile. "She will probably have strict requirements, and if I can meet all those I'll be thrilled if she will accept me as a student."

"Well, since I have no qualifications—I don't know how to play a piano, and the only singing I ever did was in church—I don't suppose I'll be studying with her, even though my grandmother was the one who invited her here," Mandie said.

"But she probably takes beginners too, or your grandmother has most likely already talked to her about you," Celia said. "Aren't you even interested in playing the piano or singing?"

"I suppose it would be nice to be able to play the piano. Everybody else in my family knows how, even Uncle John. But when would I have time to learn? Our schedule is full already," Mandie replied.

"I don't know when I'd have time either, but if Miss Marston will stay here and teach, I'll be glad to give up some free time in the afternoon," Celia said.

"Maybe I will, too," Mandie said. "But right now I want to get this homework done so I won't have to do it tomorrow."

"Me, too," Celia agreed.

When the girls had finished with their history assignment, it was time to get ready for bed. Lights had to be out by the time the curfew bell rang at ten o'clock.

Celia scrambled out of her long skirt and hung it up in the wardrobe. Then she removed her waist and put it alongside the skirt. As she put on her long nightgown, she said, "You know, Mandie, I haven't told anyone and I don't know whether anyone has noticed, but while you've been gone to the Woodards', I've been leaving the lamp burning all night to scare the rats away."

Mandie, pulling on her nightclothes, looked at her and said, "That's a good idea. And if anyone finds out, I don't see how Miss Prudence could do anything about it. After all, the workmen made the holes, we didn't."

"You're right," Celia agreed as she sat on the side of the bed.

"So we'll just keep on leaving it burning as long as those holes are in our floor," Mandie said as she jumped into bed on her side.

"That's fine with me," Celia agreed as she got under the covers on the other side of the bed.

Just then the huge bell began ringing in the backyard.

"Good night," Mandie said as she curled up.

"Good night," Celia replied. She turned over to look at the lamp on the table and drifted off to sleep.

Mandie finally dozed off with a picture of the holes in their floor in her mind. During the night, she dreamed she saw a huge rat run across their room. It seemed to be making awfully loud squeaking noises. As the rat came closer, suddenly someone was shaking her awake.

She opened her eyes. Celia was raised up on one elbow with her hand on Mandie's shoulder.

"What is it?" Mandie murmured.

"Mandie, I think there's a rat under our bed," Celia said in a nervous whisper. She moved closer to Mandie.

Mandie instantly sat up and looked around the lighted room. "A rat?" she asked softly. "I think I heard a squeak."

"I did, too, Mandie," Celia said, sliding down under the quilt.

Mandie slowly threw back the cover on her side and stepped onto the floor. She quickly stooped down, trying to see under the bed.

"Mandie, what are you doing?" Celia asked as she anxiously raised up on an elbow.

"I'm looking for the rat," Mandie said, rubbing her eyes. She couldn't see anything under the bed. The rug seemed to be in place. She was puzzled. She had definitely heard a rat. Was it in her dream? Or was it the same one Celia thought she'd heard?

"Well?" Celia questioned.

"I can't see any rat," Mandie replied as she straightened up and made a dive back into the bed.

"I'm sure I heard one," Celia told her as she lay back down.

"I did, too, but he's gone now," Mandie said, pulling the covers up around her shoulders.

"Mandie, you know what we need to do?" Celia asked.

Mandie knew what she was going to say. "Get Snowball from Grandmother's house and keep him in our room until these men get finished," she said.

"Right," Celia agreed. "That's what I was going to suggest. But do you think Miss Prudence will allow you to keep him here?"

"Remember he has stayed here before, that time we found the dead mouse," Mandie told her.

Celia shivered and said, "Yes, I remember that very well."

"Tomorrow morning I'll ask Miss Prudence if I can go over to Grandmother's house and get him," Mandie said. "I think she will allow it if we tell her we had a rat in our room."

"But, Mandie, we don't know for sure there was a rat here in our room," Celia reminded her.

"I'm sure there was, because I heard one squeaking, and you said the same thing," Mandie told her. "And Aunt Phoebe said the workmen are stirring up rats and spiders and dust and things. Remember?"

"Yes, and I suppose she has seen a rat," Celia agreed.

"I would imagine Miss Prudence might like to have Snowball around while all these holes are open, because I don't think she likes rats any better than we do," Mandie said.

"I just wish we had him in here right now. I'd sleep better," Celia said.

"If Miss Prudence agrees, I'll go over to Grandmother's right after breakfast and get him. I just hope he will stay in our room and won't run away," Mandie said.

"I'll help you look after him," Celia told her.

Mandie thought about the upsetting mess the workmen were causing. It was a long time until Thanksgiving, and they might not even be done by then. It could possibly be Christmas before they finished. How was she ever going to be able to to stand the noise, the fear of rats or even spiders, not to mention the dust the workmen stirred up.

"Good night again, Mandie," Celia said. "I hope I can go back to sleep."

"Good night," Mandie replied. "Wake me up if you hear another rat."

"You can count on that," Celia said.

"Just try to get your mind on something else, like the tea tomorrow when Tommy Patton and Robert come over from Mr. Chadwick's School," Mandie told her.

"Hmmm," Celia whispered.

The girls finally drifted off to sleep.

Chapter 7 / Unexpected Visitor

The next morning, Celia was the first to wake. She nudged Mandie and said, "Do you suppose it's safe to step out on the floor?"

Mandie sat up, looked around, and said, "Someone has already made the fire in the fireplace, so if there was a rat around, it got scared off." She slid out of bed. Celia followed.

"I wonder what they thought about our lamp still burning—whoever lit the fire," Celia remarked as she began getting her clothes together to dress.

"Oh, it was probably Aunt Phoebe, and you know she is not about to say anything that would get us in trouble," Mandie said with a shrug as she took down a dress from the tall chifferobe.

Celia hovered near the warmth of the fire as she dressed. "Are you going to ask Miss Prudence about bringing Snowball to our room?" she asked.

"As soon as we eat breakfast," Mandie replied, pulling her dress on. "I'm glad we're in the first sitting in the dining room so we can get finished early and I can catch Miss Prudence afterward." She paused and frowned, then looked at Celia and said, "I don't remember seeing Polly Cornwallis yesterday. She's still here, isn't she?"

"Oh yes, she's still going to school here. She changed to the second sitting for meals while you were gone to the Woodards' house last week. She said the first one was too early, so Miss Prudence let her change," Celia explained.

"But she wasn't in any of our classes yesterday, either," Mandie added.

"That's because she also changed her schedule. I believe she has made some friends and wanted to be in classes with them," Celia said as she buttoned up her dress.

"Oh well, I'm sure we'll see her at the social," Mandie said, brushing her shiny hair. "I'll probably wear my new red dress, the one trimmed with navy that Aunt Lou made for me," Mandie said as she quickly tied her hair back with a ribbon. She looked at Celia and smiled, adding, "Somehow that dress makes me feel all grown-up. Ready to go?"

"Ready," Celia agreed. She fluffed out her long auburn hair with one last look in the mirror.

They were the first ones in line at the dining room door. And after breakfast was over and Miss Prudence had dismissed them from the table, they were the first ones out into the hallway. Mandie hurried to catch up with Miss Prudence, who had gone on toward her office. Celia followed.

"Miss Prudence," Mandie said, coming up behind the headmistress at her office door. "May I ask you something?"

Miss Prudence turned to look at her and said,

"Why, of course, Amanda. Come on into my office." She entered the room and Mandie followed. Celia stayed outside in the corridor.

As she walked behind her desk, Miss Prudence asked, "Now what's your question, Amanda?" She sat down.

"Would you give me permission to bring Snowball over here from my grandmother's house and let him stay in our room? We think we have a rat coming out of one of those holes in the floor," Mandie spoke fast.

"A rat? Oh dear! Did y'all see a rat in your room?" Miss Prudence visibly shivered at the thought.

"We woke up during the night, and I heard a rat squeak somewhere; so we got up and looked around, and the noise stopped. So he must have gone back out one of the holes," Mandie explained.

"You know it's against my rules to have a cat in the house," Miss Prudence said, hesitating.

"Yes, ma'am, but we've never had holes in the floor and the walls before, either," Mandie reminded her.

"Under the circumstances," Miss Prudence began, and she paused to look at Mandie, "I suppose it would be permissible to bring the cat here, but you must keep him *in* your room. He is not to roam the house or disturb the other girls. Do you understand, Amanda?"

"Yes, ma'am, thank you, Miss Prudence," Mandie replied with a smile. "The only time he'll be out of my room is when I take him outdoors for exercise."

"All right, now I believe Uncle Cal is going to the depot this morning to pick up a package that came

in for me on the train. You may go with him and de-
tour by your grandmother's house to get the cat,"
Miss Prudence told her.

"Oh, thank you, Miss Prudence! I'll go find him,"
Mandie said as she started to leave the room.

"Amanda, don't forget. We are having guests today. You need to get this errand over with so you will
be ready for the tea this afternoon," Miss Prudence
reminded her.

"Yes, ma'am," Mandie said as she rushed out of
the room and found Celia waiting just down the hallway.

"What did she say?" Celia asked.

"I have permission to go with Uncle Cal when he
picks up something at the depot, and then we'll go
by Grandmother's and get Snowball. Come on. I
have to find Uncle Cal," Mandie told her.

They found Uncle Cal in the kitchen. He was
Aunt Phoebe's husband, and they lived in the little
cottage in the backyard of the school. He had just
finished his breakfast and was telling Phoebe he
planned to leave shortly.

"I has to git somethin' from de depot fo' Miz Prudence, and I might as well git on and git it," he was
saying.

As Mandie and Celia walked down to the far end
of the long kitchen where he and Aunt Phoebe were
talking, Mandie said, "I want to go with you, Uncle
Cal. Miss Prudence said I could bring Snowball over
here because of the rats and that you could take me
by Grandmother's house to get him."

"Dat be a right good idea," Aunt Phoebe said.
"Maybe he catch all de rats in dis heah house. I fix
de sandbox fo' him whilst you gone."

"And I'll help," Celia said.

Uncle Cal started out the door, and Mandie followed. She turned back to say, "Thanks, Celia, I should have asked Miss Prudence if you could ride with us over there."

"Hurry back," Celia called to her.

"I will," Mandie promised.

Uncle Cal drove by the depot and picked up a huge box for Miss Prudence. Mandie wondered what could be in it. It barely fit into the back of the rig.

"Where did that box come from, Uncle Cal?" Mandie asked as a workman at the depot helped him load it.

"Miz Prudence, she say she ask fo' de box from Noo Yawk," the old man replied as he got back into the rig.

"New York," Mandie repeated. "I wonder what she is getting from up there."

Uncle Cal shook the reins and drove on down the street. "Might be books," he said as they traveled along the cobblestone street. "Most books come from Noo Yawk."

"I suppose it could be just books. I thought maybe it might be something really interesting," Mandie said with a big sigh.

Mrs. Taft wasn't home but Annie was. She helped Mandie round up Snowball. Uncle Cal waited in the driveway with the rig.

Mandie hurried through the house calling, "Snowball, Snowball. Where are you? Come here, Snowball." Annie followed.

"Oh, where is that cat?" Mandie asked as they glanced into rooms along the way—and there were lots of rooms in the huge mansion.

"Upstairs mebbe," Annie said.

"Oh sure, he's piled up on my bed, fast asleep,"

Mandie said, laughing as she raced up the steps and down the corridor to the room she claimed for her own when she stayed with her grandmother. The door was slightly open, and Mandie gave it a push to look inside. There was the white cat, curled up on her bed. He looked at her, stood up on the counterpane, and stretched.

"He not been heah long 'cause I give him breakfast li'l while ago," the young maid told Mandie.

Mandie reached over and picked him up. "Let me get your leash," she told him as she took down the red leash hanging on a hook by the tall wardrobe. She hooked it onto his collar and set him down to walk. "Now let's go."

Snowball had learned a long time ago that when Mandie put his leash on, they were going outside. He tried to run down the stairs to the front door, but Mandie kept a firm hold on the leash to slow him down.

"Annie, would you please tell Grandmother that Miss Prudence gave me permission to come and get Snowball because of the rats in the schoolhouse?" Mandie asked her.

"Lawsy mercy, you dun got rats in de schoolhouse!" Annie said with a loud gasp.

"They may be coming out of the holes in the walls and the floors," Mandie explained. "I'm sure Celia and I heard one in our room last night, but when we got up and looked we couldn't see anything."

"Do be careful," Annie told Mandie as Mandie hurried to get into the rig with Uncle Cal. Mandie waved back at the young girl.

When Mandie got back to the schoolhouse, she brought Snowball upstairs and set him down in her and Celia's room. The cat immediately ran around the room sniffing and then lay down and scratched at the rug over the hole in the floor.

"He knows there's a hole under that rug," Mandie told Celia as the two watched him. "He probably smells a rat."

"And he may manage to pull the rug off the hole," Celia added. "I think I'll sleep better tonight with him in the room."

"So will I, because I know if a rat dares enter this room Snowball will make a meal of him," Mandie said with a laugh.

At the noon meal, Miss Prudence made an announcement. She took her place at the head of the long table while the girls filed into the room and stood behind their chairs.

The headmistress picked up her little silver bell by her plate and shook it, making it tinkle softly. "Young ladies," she said. "I must trust you all to be on your best behavior, and I will leave you alone for the meal. Our special guest, Miss Marston, has arrived, and Miss Hope and I will be dining with her in our living quarters. Aunt Pheobe and Millie will be in and out of the room here while you enjoy your food, and they will give me a report on your conduct. Now please be seated. I will see you all at tea this afternoon." She motioned for them to sit down.

As the girls took their places at the table, Miss Prudence left the dining room. The students all looked at each other, but even without Miss Prudence's presence they didn't dare speak a word. Conversation was always forbidden during mealtime.

Mandie and Celia, who sat next to each other, hurried through their meal and had to wait for some of the others to finish. Then Aunt Phoebe walked up to the head of the table and said, "Miz Prudence say y'all dismissed when you gits done eatin'."

Without a word, all the pupils hurried out of the room, but once they stepped into the hallway, conversation began. And most of it was about the tea that was being held that afternoon.

"I should take Snowball out for a walk," Mandie told Celia as they paused in the corridor. "I'll give him something to eat after the tea."

"All right," Celia said as they started for the stairs. "Where are you going to feed him, Mandie?"

"Don't you worry none 'bout dat," Aunt Phoebe said as she came up behind them. "I bring him down to de kitchen aftuh a while and give him something to eat. Y'all jes' do de exercisin', I do de feedin', and I sho hopes he ketch a rat or two."

Mandie and Celia had stopped and turned around when the woman spoke. "Oh, thank you, Aunt Phoebe, and I hope he catches some rats, too," Mandie told her. "And thanks for putting the sandbox in our room for him. We're going to take him outside now. Then we'll come back and begin getting ready for the tea."

The girls opened the door to their room and found Snowball crouching over the hole in the floor. He had pulled the rug away and was so intent on whatever he could smell that he ignored Mandie when she spoke to him.

"Snowball, come on, we're going outside for a little while," she said as she stooped to push him away and pull the rug back in place. Snowball finally looked up at his mistress and made growling sounds as though he were trying to talk.

Celia laughed and said, "He doesn't like that. He

probably smelled a rat down that hole."

"Too bad, because right now he's got to go outside," Mandie said, reaching for his leash on the bureau and snapping it onto his collar.

The girls took the cat out for a walk in the yard. Mandie held tightly to his leash so he could not run away. Mornings and nights were cool now with autumn weather, but the middle of the day was warm in the sunshine.

"I suppose Miss Prudence will have the tea inside the house even though it is warm enough to be outdoors," Mandie remarked.

"I would imagine so," Celia replied. "For one thing, Miss Marston will probably play the piano for us or sing, and she would have to do that inside."

"I wonder if my grandmother is coming over for the tea," Mandie said as they walked about. "Since she was the one who got Miss Marston to come, I suppose she will be here. And that could spell trouble. You heard that remark April Snow made to me about my grandmother and that 'music business,' as she called it."

"I doubt that April would do anything to make trouble with your grandmother or Miss Marston while they're here. Miss Prudence would really punish her if she tried anything," Celia said, reaching up to pull a dried leaf from the huge magnolia tree they were walking under. She split it into small pieces as they continued through the yard.

"But you know April Snow. She never seems to give a hoot whether she gets into trouble or not. In fact she always looks as if she enjoys it," Mandie replied. She tightened her grip on the leash to slow Snowball down as he tried to rush ahead.

"Well, I hope April Snow behaves herself this afternoon," Celia replied.

They walked down the long driveway and were almost to the road when someone called Mandie's name. Mandie quickly stopped and looked back. Polly Cornwallis was hurrying toward them.

"Mandie, Miss Prudence wants to see you," Polly called to her as she got closer.

Mandie and Celia came to meet her. "Miss Prudence wants to see me?" Mandie asked as they caught up with each other.

"Yes, and she said right now," Polly told her. She tossed her long dark hair as she looked at Mandie with eyes that were as dark as chinquapins.

"Right now? I wonder what she wants," Mandie said as the three slowly began the uphill walk to the front steps.

"I have no idea. She just now stopped me in the hallway and said, 'Go find Amanda,' and I happened to see you and Celia go outside with Snowball a little while ago," Polly explained.

"It must be important, whatever it is," Celia commented.

"I suppose, but I can't imagine what she wants," Mandie said as they reached the front porch.

Polly went ahead and opened the front door. Celia reached for Snowball's leash. "Let me have Snowball, Mandie. I'll take him on up to our room," she said.

Mandie gave her the end of the leash and said, "I should be up shortly. That is, if I am not in trouble about something." She frowned.

"I'll see y'all after while," Polly called back as she hurried up the staircase in the front hallway. Celia followed.

Mandie walked toward Miss Prudence's office. She stopped outside the doorway and looked in. The headmistress was sitting behind her desk.

"Come on in, Amanda," Miss Prudence invited her. "This will only take a minute."

"Yes, ma'am," Mandie said as she stepped inside to stand before the desk. She watched Miss Prudence closely.

"Amanda, as you know, your grandmother arranged for Miss Marston to come to our school, and we are very grateful," Miss Prudence began as she looked at Mandie across her desk. "However, we have an unexpected situation that affects you." She paused.

Mandie's heart beat faster. What had she done now? She was silent.

"It seems that Dr. Woodard has returned to your grandmother's house for a rest on his way to see other patients, and he has his son, Joe, with him," Miss Prudence explained as she again paused to look at Mandie.

"Oh, but, Miss Prudence, my grandmother has always welcomed Dr. Woodard when he comes to town," Mandie said with a sigh of relief.

"But, Amanda, this time Mrs. Taft has invited the doctor and his son to our tea this afternoon, and since Joe is not one of Mr. Chadwick's students, I'm afraid you will have to entertain him or he will feel left out, so to speak," Miss Prudence said.

"That's fine, Miss Prudence," Mandie said, wondering what the headmistress's concern was.

"Therefore, that means you will have to spend your time conversing with Joe rather than the young Patton fellow you always pair off with," the lady told her.

Suddenly Mandie realized what Miss Prudence was explaining. She had looked forward to seeing Tommy Patton again, but now Joe had suddenly appeared in town. She would have to talk to Joe instead of Tommy during the tea. She drew a deep breath as she had another thought—one of the other girls might take over Tommy! He was by far the best-looking in Mr. Chadwick's School, and she knew other girls had been envious of her.

"Amanda, do you understand what I am saying?" Miss Prudence asked her sharply.

"Oh yes, ma'am" Mandie said, blowing out her breath. "I will talk to Joe Woodard at the tea."

"I will see that another girl is paired off with Thomas Patton. Now you may go," Miss Prudence said as she rose behind her desk.

"Yes, ma'am, Miss Prudence," Mandie said as she turned and left the office.

Her footsteps dragged on the way to her room as she thought about the situation. Why had her grandmother invited Dr. Woodard and Joe to the tea? She was not happy with the sudden arrangement.

When she got to her room and told Celia what the summons to the office was all about, Celia was practically speechless with surprise.

"Grandmother knows I always see Tommy Patton at the teas we have. I don't know why she did this," Mandie complained as she walked about the room.

"I suppose she wanted to attend and, since Joe and his father were at her house, she felt obligated to bring them, Mandie," Celia tried to console her.

Mandie suddenly stood still and frowned. "Maybe April Snow is right. My grandmother is taking over the running of this school," she said.

"Mandie, let's lay our clothes out and start getting ready," Celia told her.

Mandie bit her lip and said, "Why should I get all dressed up for Joe? He's seen me in my old gingham dresses."

"Oh, but that's the reason you should get dressed up," Celia said. "To show Joe how beautiful you can be."

Mandie shrugged and followed Celia to the chifferobe to take down the dress she was going to wear. The excitement of the tea had been dulled for her.

Chapter 8 / Tea Time

Mandie put on her new red dress, piled her long blond hair on top of her head, and pinned a bow in it to match the navy trimming around the neckline and the hemline. As she hooked the chain holding her gold locket around her neck, she opened it and looked at the picture of her father inside. He would have been proud of his daughter in all this finery, she was sure. *Oh, if only he could have lived to be an old man, to see me grow up*, she thought.

Celia glanced at her as she walked over to stand before the long mirror in the corner of their room. "I know what you're thinking," she told Mandie. "I'm thinking the same thing about my father, if he could see me now. Most fathers live to see their children grow up at least, but that horse . . . put an end to it." Her voice was full of emotion.

"At least we still have our mothers," Mandie reminded her as she closed the cover on her locket.

"Yes, and I'm thankful for that," Celia replied as

she brushed her long auburn hair. Her pink silk dress gave a slight reflection in her green eyes.

Snowball was curled up asleep on the bed, and Mandie made sure the door was tightly closed as they left the room. The two girls joined the other students down in the two parlors. Everyone was standing and talking.

As Mandie and Celia paused at the doorway of the small parlor to look inside, Miss Hope hurried through the crowd, talking as she walked, "Young ladies, please find seats. Mr. Chadwick and his boys will be here any minute now."

As there was a scramble for seats, Mandie looked for her grandmother and Dr. Woodard and Joe. Miss Hope, in her best black dress, stood in the center of the room as she announced, "This tea will be informal, and we expect you older girls to pair off with the older boys you all know from Mr. Chadwick's School. Our new pupils this year will engage in social conversation with his first-year boys. I understand his school is overflowing and has a larger number of boys than we have girls. Therefore, Mr. Chadwick is only bringing as many boys as we have girls." She paused to look around the room. "Are there any questions?"

"Please tell me just what an informal tea is?" April Snow asked from a far corner of the room. A snicker went through the crowd.

"Young ladies, you are supposed to be on your best manners today, and that giggle was very unladylike," Miss Hope reprimanded the group. Then, looking at April, she replied, "We will just talk and sit around and drink tea. There will be no grades given for the tea today because we will have Miss Marston playing and perhaps singing for us. Does that answer your question, April?"

April Snow just shrugged, without replying, and turned her gaze in the other direction. Mandie looked the same way and saw her grandmother, Dr. Woodard, and Joe going down the hall outside the doorway. Joe was wearing his Sunday-go-to-meeting suit. His father always dressed in a suit, and Mrs. Taft, of course, was wearing her best.

"Did you see them?" Mandie whispered to Celia.

"Yes," Celia whispered back. "I wonder where they are going and why they didn't come in here."

"They are probably going wherever Miss Prudence is, to meet Miss Marston," Mandie told her.

At that moment Mr. Chadwick and his students arrived. The boys formed a line down the hallway to the parlor door. Each one had been given a slip of paper with a girl's name on it, and as they stepped up to the doorway they announced the names.

Robert was among the first, and he smiled broadly and said, "Miss Celia Hamilton."

Celia smiled back and crossed the room to greet him as she told Mandie, "I'll explain to Robert just in case you don't get a chance to speak to Tommy."

"Thanks," Mandie replied as she continued watching the doorway. She was beginning to wonder if Tommy Patton had come with the other students when he appeared and called Etrulia Batson's name. She watched as Etrulia rose from the other side of the room and joined him at the doorway. He never did seem to catch Mandie's glance. He and Etrulia followed the other couples across the hall to the larger parlor. Mandie felt so jealous of Etrulia she didn't pay any attention to the other students.

Suddenly she realized she was alone in the

room. The students had all moved on out through the huge hallway into the other parlor.

"Where is Joe Woodard? Here I sit like a nin-compoop, all by myself," she said as she rose, shook out the folds in her long skirts, and started toward the door.

Before she reached the hallway, Joe came rush-ing into the room. "Sorry, Mandie," he said. "But I was told to wait until all the students had got paired off before I could come and speak to you." He paused to look directly at Mandie. "My, my, you look absolutely beautiful! I'm sure I got the prettiest girl in the class."

"Oh, Joe, you look so handsome!" Mandie teased back with a big smile.

"Well, where's the food?" Joe asked as he looked around the huge room.

"You know very well this is a tea, and you will only be served a cup of awful-tasting tea and one little tea biscuit," Mandie replied with a grin. "Too bad you had to get all dressed up just for that."

"But I didn't get dressed up for that. I got dressed to come visit you," he replied as they stood there in the middle of the floor.

Mandie didn't know what to reply, but right then the other students began drifting back into the room.

"I think we'd better get seats while we can. Some of us will have to stand because this parlor is small but it has the piano over there," Mandie told him as she led the way to the far corner of the room. They sat down on a small settee there.

As soon as all the seats were taken and the other students had found a place to stand, the maids came in with trays and began serving. As the two accepted tea and biscuits, Mandie whispered to Joe, "We are not being graded today, so I'll be glad to give you my tea if you want it."

Joe looked at her and said, "And I'll be glad to give you my tea if you want it. Why don't they at least give you a choice of tea or coffee?" He looked at the cup and saucer in his hand.

"Because it wouldn't be a tea if they didn't serve tea. Joe Woodard, I've seen you drink tea before," Mandie said as she held her cup and saucer.

"Only when I have to," Joe said. "And I suppose this is one of those have-to times." He suddenly raised his cup and smelled the liquid in it. He quickly looked at Mandie. "Try yours."

Mandie frowned but finally tasted the brown liquid. Her blue eyes opened wide as she told him, "This is coffee! Somebody will get in trouble when Miss Prudence finds out what we're drinking."

"We'd better drink it up before Miss Prudence tells us to pour it out, then," Joe said with a grin as he drank heartily from his cup.

"Yes," Mandie agreed as she took a bite of her biscuit and then drank the coffee.

Miss Prudence entered the room with a tall, beautiful brunette woman. She looked to be in her late thirties, Mandie thought. Mrs. Taft and Dr. Woodard followed. Mandie watched as the headmistress indicated where her grandmother and the doctor should sit and then directed Miss Marston to the piano.

As the others sat down, Miss Prudence stepped over to a small table and spoke. "Young ladies, young gentlemen, we are grateful to have Miss Marston with us today. While you all have your tea, Miss Marston will play," she announced as Miss Marston adjusted the piano stool. "And I might explain that your tea today is actually coffee in honor of our special guest—Miss Marston does not drink tea. Now here's Miss Marston."

As the pianist struck the first chords of the Blue Danube Waltz, Mandie grinned at Joe and whispered, "I was not interested in Miss Marston before, but now I like her. She drinks coffee."

During the performance, Mandie kept glancing around the room in search of Tommy Patton, but if he was in the parlor he was not within her range of vision. When the music ended and Miss Prudence took the floor again, Mandie became interested in hearing what she was saying, because Uncle Cal was carrying in the large box he had picked up at the depot.

"We have been given a great opportunity for you music lovers," Miss Prudence was saying. "Miss Marston has agreed to stay with us until at least the first of the year, and she will add music lessons to our curriculum." She paused. The group was entirely silent, so she continued, "Now, Uncle Cal, if you would please set that box on the table there." She indicated a long table at the side and then said, "Young ladies, please form a line and take a music book from the box. We will be using these books with our lessons."

Mandie sighed and Joe grinned at her as they stood up. Then he tried to act serious and said, "Mandie, you know in order to be a lady you need to be accomplished in music."

"I don't want to be a lady, not the kind Miss Prudence expects us to be," Mandie told him as she moved toward the line.

"But it's nice to be able to play a piano for your

own enjoyment," Joe said.

"Nice for you because your mother taught piano," Mandie reminded him as she fell in behind the last girl and Joe sat back down.

Mandie was thinking to herself, *What a miserable day!* when she heard Celia calling to her. She looked up and saw her friend ahead in the line.

"Mandie," Celia said as she stepped back to join Mandie. "Isn't this a wonderful opportunity for us?"

"Oh, Celia, you know I'm not really interested when there are other things I'd much rather get involved in," Mandie replied.

"Yes, I know," Celia replied. "Robert and I have been sitting across the hallway, through the double doors there in the other parlor. Everyone couldn't get in here without being stepped on."

"Is Tommy in there, too?" Mandie asked.

"He and Etrulia Batson are sitting near us, but we haven't been talking to them. For one thing, Etrulia sure has a busy tongue, and Tommy seems to devour every word," Celia replied.

Mandie frowned and didn't answer as they moved on.

"Don't worry, Mandie," Celia said. "I believe Etrulia is one of those women that men just don't know what to do with them, and Tommy is just full of curiosity and doesn't know how to react to all that talking she is doing."

Mandie still didn't reply.

As they reached the table with the box of books, Mandie took one and said, "Uncle Cal thought there might be books in the box when we picked it up at the depot on the way to Grandmother's house." Celia picked up a book and looked inside as they move on, but Mandie didn't even open hers.

"I have to go back to Robert," Celia said. "If I hear anything interesting, I'll tell you about it later."

"And I have to go back to Joe," Mandie said with a sigh.

When everyone had taken a book from the box and returned to their places, Miss Prudence spoke again. "Young ladies, you are now free to spend the rest of the day in whatever way you choose. Just be sure you bring the music books to your first class Monday, and we will set up a schedule for music lessons. You are dismissed."

Mr. Chadwick immediately spoke from the doorway. "Young men, we will now return to our school. Please bid the young ladies goodbye and assemble on the front lawn for transportation."

Mandie sat with Joe, silently watching as the room emptied out, and the sound of conversation drifted away. She looked around and saw that Miss Marston, Miss Prudence, Miss Hope, her grandmother, and Joe's father had also left.

"Let's sit in the swing on the front porch," Mandie told Joe as they stood up.

As they started toward the door, Mandie looked down at the book in her hands and said, "If you don't mind, I'll take this up to my room, and I'll be right back."

"Of course, Mandie, go ahead. I'll wait for you on the porch," Joe replied as he continued toward the front door.

Mandie rushed up the stairs and found Celia had returned to their room.

"Is Joe gone already?" Celia asked as she turned away from the window where she had been watching the boys drive away in their rigs.

"No, he's waiting for me on the porch. Why

don't you come on down and join us?'' Mandie said as she placed the music book on the bureau. She felt something was wrong, and then she suddenly remembered. Quickly looking around the room, she asked, "Where is Snowball?"

"Oh, Snowball!" Celia said with a loud gasp. "I don't remember seeing him when I came in just now."

The two girls quickly searched under the bed, inside the tall chifferobe, and every place where the cat might be. Snowball was definitely missing.

"Celia, I have to find Snowball. There's no telling where he went," Mandie told her friend.

"I'll help you, Mandie," Celia said. "But where could he be?"

Mandie thought for a moment, and then she said, "First I'll see if Aunt Phoebe has taken him down to the kitchen to eat. Come on."

The girls hurried downstairs and back to the kitchen where Aunt Phoebe and the extra maids were cleaning up after the tea.

"Now what fo' y'all in such a hurry?" the old woman asked as she looked up from the dishes she was stacking on the table.

"Snowball, Aunt Phoebe, is he down here?" Mandie asked as she and Celia quickly looked around the room.

"I ain't seed him, not since dis mawnin' when you brang him from yo' grandmother's. In fact, I was jes' afixin' to go git him and give him a bite to eat," Aunt Phoebe explained as she wiped her hands on her large white apron.

"Somehow he got out of our room, Aunt Phoebe," Mandie said. Turning to Celia, she asked, "Was the door closed when you went in?"

"It was closed. I remember thinking I should be sure to close it behind me when I went inside so he couldn't get out," Celia replied.

Mandie stomped her foot and said, "Oh, shucks! I suppose I'll have to spend the rest of the day looking for him. I just hope Miss Prudence doesn't find out he's running around loose somewhere."

"Y'all jes' don't tell huh 'less she asks," Aunt Phoebe advised. "If you don't find him soon, let me know, and I'll git Cal to he'p."

"Thanks, Aunt Phoebe," Mandie said.

"With all those students going and coming, someone could have let him outside, Mandie," Celia said as they turned to leave the kitchen.

"I know," Mandie agreed. "So I suppose we should start down here to look for him and then work our way upstairs."

As they left the kitchen and started down the hallway, Mandie remembered that Joe was waiting. "I'd better let Joe know," she said as she walked toward the front door.

When she and Celia stepped outside onto the front porch and Mandie told Joe, he grinned and said, "That's to be expected from that cat. You know he loves to run away."

Mandie frowned and said, "I don't know where my grandmother and your father are right now, but I sure hope Snowball doesn't find them."

"You girls look for Snowball, and I'll look for the adults and try to keep them out of your way," Joe said with a laugh.

"All right, we'll catch up with you in a little while," Mandie told him.

They all went inside the house. Joe walked toward Miss Prudence's office, and Mandie and Celia circled in the opposite direction to search the parlors and classrooms. They looked under all the furniture and in all the closets and cabinets.

Their search took a long time. The schoolhouse was big because it had once been a huge mansion and had been converted into the present school. There were currently forty girls living there and the two mistresses, Miss Prudence and Miss Hope, had their private quarters on the first floor. Mandie and Celia shared a small room on the third floor.

So it took a while to cover the whole house in their search. They even tried the attic door, but it was latched, and Mandie knew Snowball could not have gone in there. Since they had on their fancy dresses and the attic was usually full of dust, they didn't go inside.

"He has to be somewhere," Mandie said with a loud moan as they stood at the top of the steps to the attic.

"Do you suppose he has gone into Miss Prudence's part of the house?" Celia asked.

"I sure hope not. But you know we can't go into all the girls' rooms to look for him, so he could be in one of those," Mandie replied as they descended the stairs. "Let's look around the first floor again. He might have smelled food and found his way down there."

The two girls went through the rooms on the first floor again and finally ended up in the parlor.

"He must be outside," Mandie said with a sigh.

Celia walked over to the baby grand piano. "I'd love to take lessons on this," she said as she ran her fingers down the keyboard, causing a few keys to strike.

Mandie was watching her when suddenly she

heard a growl and saw Snowball jump out of the piano. She quickly grabbed him and said, "He was inside the piano!" She bent to look under the raised lid. "I hope he didn't damage something."

Celia looked, too, and said, "I don't think he did."

"Of all the places to hide," Mandie said, frowning as she held tightly to the cat. "I might as well take him to Aunt Phoebe so she can feed him while he's down here."

"He must like music," Celia said with a giggle.

"But he couldn't have been in there when Miss Marston played," Mandie said as they started down the hallway. "Why don't you see if you can find Joe and let him know we found Snowball? Then we can all go out on the porch."

"All right, we'll meet you there," Celia said as she continued toward Miss Prudence's quarters, and Mandie went on to the kitchen.

Mandie pushed open the door and announced, "Here he is, Aunt Phoebe, and you'll never guess where he was."

Aunt Phoebe stopped drying dishes to look at her. "In Miz Prudence's rooms?"

"Oh no, thank goodness," Mandie replied. "He was inside the piano."

The other maids paused in their work to listen to Mandie's description of her and Celia's search.

"You jes' leave dat cat wid me, and I'll feed him," the old woman told her.

Mandie looked around the kitchen and asked, "How are you going to keep him from running out when someone opens the door?"

"I feeds him in de broom closet, and I shuts de do'," Aunt Phoebe explained.

Mandie frowned and asked, "You shut him up in the closet?"

"Oh, but dat closet it's got a window," Aunt Phoebe explained. "He ain't gwine smother in dere." She reached for Snowball, who seemed glad to change hands.

"Thank you, Aunt Phoebe," Mandie said. "Then you'll put him back in our room, won't you?"

"Dat I'll do," the woman replied as she started toward the broom closet with Snowball.

"I appreciate it," Mandie said. "I'm sorry to cause you so much trouble."

The woman paused to look at her and, with a loud grunt, she said, "Humph! Ain't no trouble. But you ain't like yo' mother. Miz 'Lizbeth, when she went to school heah. She always quiet. Nobody ever know she 'bout. But you, Missy 'Manda, you keep us happy wid all de excitement. Now you go 'head and see dat Joe boy. I tend to dis heah cat." She opened the door to the closet and put Snowball inside and then closed the door.

"Thanks," Mandie said with a big smile as she blew a kiss to the woman and went on out the door in search of her friends.

Mandie found them on the front porch. She joined Joe in the swing as Celia sat in a rocker nearby.

"Whew!" she said. "He's all taken care of. Joe, did you learn anything new from the adults that we ought to know?"

"Not much, except that Miss Marston will not be here all the time—every day, that is—because she has engagements for the season and will be teaching here in-between," Joe replied.

"I just thought of something," Mandie told her

friends. "How is Miss Marston going to teach music when those workmen are always hammering and making so much noise that we can't even hear half the teacher says?"

Celia thought about that for a moment and said, "I have an idea Miss Prudence will demand that they be quiet while Miss Marston is teaching."

"Is it really that bad?" Joe asked.

"Terrible. You should be here to hear it," Mandie replied. "I can't wait to see how Miss Prudence will solve that problem."

And she didn't have long to wait because Miss Prudence made an announcement at supper that night. And Mandie didn't like what she had to say.

Chapter 9 / Disappeared!

At supper that night, Miss Prudence brought all the adults with her to dine with the girls. Joe sat next to his father, with Mrs. Taft and Miss Marston at the head of the table, beside the headmistress.

After they were all seated, Miss Prudence tinkled the little silver bell she kept by her place and made an announcement.

"Young ladies," she began, "we have had a conference this afternoon and Mrs. Taft has volunteered the use of one of her parlors and pianos for you students here who will be taking lessons from Miss Marston, since, as you all know, the workmen have to make all that noise to install the furnace and the electric lights."

Mandie didn't like this idea at all. Her grandmother's house was practically her home while she attended school, and the idea of all these other girls invading it upset her. She felt Celia squeeze her hand under the edge of the white linen tablecloth.

"No!" Mandie said under her breath. She didn't want all these girls traipsing through her grandmother's house.

"We will begin lessons on Monday with the entire group assembled in the chapel for an introduction to music. Then we will set up a schedule, and Uncle Cal will drive you girls to and from Mrs. Taft's house for lessons," Miss Prudence continued.

Mandie felt everyone looking at her. She could almost hear what they were thinking. Her grandmother was getting too involved in running the school.

As soon as supper was over, the girls were dismissed, but Miss Prudence stopped Mandie and Celia as they started to leave the dining room.

"Amanda, your grandmother has asked permission for you and Celia Hamilton to spend tonight at her house since Dr. Woodard and his son Joe will be there," Miss Prudence told her. "If you two would like to do that, you may go."

"Oh yes, ma'am," Mandie said as she looked ahead for Joe, who was stepping into the hallway.

"And so would I, Miss Prudence," Celia added.

"Then, make sure you return in time for supper tomorrow night," Miss Prudence told them, and she went to join Miss Marston who was waiting for her at the doorway.

Ben, Mrs. Taft's driver, was waiting with her rig and took her, Dr. Woodard, Joe, Mandie, and Celia to her house. The only talk about music that night was Mrs. Taft telling Mandie she would have to begin piano lessons.

After they were in their room for the night, Mandie said to Celia, "I suppose I'll have to take piano lessons. I have to do whatever Grandmother decides. It's impossible to change her mind."

"But, Mandie, I think you'll like piano lessons after you get started," Celia told her as she dressed for bed. "I remember I didn't want to take lessons, either, when I was small, but now I'm glad I can play, and I want to go on with my music. I want to get better and maybe even make a career of it."

Mandie kicked off her slippers as she jumped into bed and said, "Like Miss Marston?"

"I'd like to try for that, but I don't know whether I could ever be that good or not," Celia said as she got in on the other side of the big bed.

Snowball jumped up on top of the cover and curled up at Mandie's feet.

"Oh, Celia, I'm sure you can do it if that's what you want, but somehow I can't picture you as a pianist," Mandie told her. "Maybe a teacher, but not a pianist."

"But, Mandie, I would like to teach, too, like Miss Marston is doing," Celia said.

"Well, I suppose my grandmother has it all cut out for me to manage the family business when I grow up," Mandie said. "But you know what I'd like to do. I'd like to live out in the country and farm and have lots of animals around."

Celia sighed and said, "We'll probably both change our minds a few times before we're old enough to do such things. And we both may end up old married women."

Mandie quickly turned over to protest. "Not me," she said. "First of all, I want to do things and go places. I don't want to get married and settle down in one place. I want to see the world, see how other people live. And then I'd like to live in the country."

"Well, you could begin by going to New York with me and my mother," Celia told her. "Don't forget to write and ask your mother if you can go."

Mandie suddenly jumped out of bed, turned up the lamp, and said, "I'm going to do that right now." She got a pen and paper out of the desk in the room and quickly scribbled a letter to her mother.

"Tell her I asked you to go, and I know my mother would want you to go with us, too. I'm sure she trusts my mother to take good care of you. After all, your mother and my mother went to school together and have known each other all these years," Celia said as she sat up in bed and watched Mandie. "And we could go visit Jonathan Guyer."

"Oh yes, we'd have to go see Jonathan," Mandie said as she folded the paper, put it into an envelope, addressed it, and licked it to seal it. "Now all I have to do is give this to Ben, and he will mail it for me." She laid the letter on the bureau and then turned down the lamp before jumping back into bed.

———

Sunday after the noon meal, Dr. Woodard and Joe left on their way home. Soon after that, Mandie and Celia took Snowball and returned to school.

After supper at school, Mandie and Celia went back up to their room to catch up with some studying before they crawled into bed for the night.

Monday morning, in accordance with Miss Prudence's order, the girls in the school gathered in the chapel. Miss Marston gave them a lecture on the basics of music, but only a few in the group seemed really interested.

"Now if you will all study the first chapter in your

music books, we will begin with scales tomorrow when we go to Mrs. Taft's house for our first lesson," Miss Marston told them. "Miss Prudence has said we will make these sessions short so all the girls who desire to study music may begin with their lessons."

Desire! Mandie thought. *She should have said, "all the girls who were required to study music."* Celia had taken in every word Miss Marston had to say. Evidently Miss Prudence had held the workmen off until Miss Marston was finished, because once the girls began leaving the chapel the loud noises began in furious rapidity.

Mandie had not run into Etrulia Batson since Saturday, until that morning. Talking was not permitted except in the hallways and as Mandie and Celia stepped into the corridor, Etrulia, who was ahead of them, turned back to speak.

"Mandie, did you know Tommy Patton has an ancestor who was a pirate? Tommy told me all about him. He used to rob ships off the coast of Charleston," Etrulia said.

Mandie stopped and looked at the girl. "That's not so," she said. "He had sea captains in his family. I've been to his house in Charleston, and I've seen their portraits."

Etrulia looked at her sharply and said, "He plainly told me he had a pirate ancestor. His name was something-or-other Grey. I can't remember the first name."

Suddenly April Snow, who was immediately in front of Etrulia, turned around and said, "He did not. My ancestor who was a pirate was named Grey."

"Well, then, maybe you're kin," Celia spoke up with a big laugh.

"I'm no kin to that snob," April said loudly as she pushed her way ahead in the crowd of girls who had stopped to listen to the conversation.

Etrulia started to walk on, but Mandie called to her, "I think you'd better ask Tommy exactly what he did tell you. I'm sure he doesn't have an ancestor who was a pirate."

"Humph!" Etrulia muttered as she glanced back and kept on going.

Mandie stomped her foot and said, "Well then, I'll ask him myself—whenever I see him again."

"I think it would be awfully intriguing to have a pirate in the family genealogy," Celia said as they continued down the hallway. "And according to history there were lots of pirates back in the old days, so there must be quite a few people who have descended from them."

"I've never known anyone kin to a pirate," Mandie told her as they came to the doorway of their next class and entered the room.

At noontime the girls quickly ran to their room, left their books, and freshened up. Snowball roamed around the room, rubbing against Mandie's ankles and purring.

"Snowball, what are you talking about?" Mandie teased him as she stooped and rubbed his head, which caused him to look up at her with his blue eyes and start meowing loudly. "I know. You're probably begging for food. It won't be long now before Aunt Phoebe comes to get you. And I know she'll have lots for you to eat. You behave now." She stood up.

Celia looked at her and smiled as she asked, "Do you really believe Snowball understands what you say?"

Mandie laughed and said, "I just pretend he does, and he pretends I can understand him. Let's go."

The girls quickly left the room. Mandie was sure to shut the door before Snowball could follow. They raced down the stairs to get in line at the dining room.

Miss Prudence set the time limit at the table. The girls all had learned that when the headmistress was finished with her food the meal was over, so they usually hurried.

Mandie and Celia rushed back to their room to get their books for the next class after the noon meal. As they opened the door, Mandie noticed the rug over the hole in the floor had been pushed back into a pile.

"Snowball must have done this," she said as she bent to straighten the rug and cover the hole. She looked around the room. "And Aunt Phoebe must have already come up and got him to go eat."

"Probably," Celia agreed as she quickly pinned back a fly-away wisp of hair. "Ready?" She picked up her books.

"Ready," Mandie agreed as she grabbed her books from a chair.

They had two classes after the noon meal each day and were then usually free for the rest of the day to study or take care of other things, unless Miss Prudence added something extra now and then. So after Mandie and Celia finished their two classes that afternoon, they returned to their room.

Mandie cautiously opened the door as she watched for her cat, who was always ready to make an escape. She stepped inside as Celia followed.

"Snowball, where are you?" Mandie said as she

looked about the room. She quickly flipped up the bed ruffle and looked beneath as she called, "Snowball."

Celia helped her look. There was no cat to be found.

"He's not here," Mandie said as she stood in the middle of the room.

"Maybe Aunt Phoebe has him down in the kitchen," Celia said.

"I'd better go see," Mandie said with a loud sigh. "I'll be right back."

But when Mandie found Aunt Phoebe in the kitchen, the woman was puzzled.

"I goes up to git him to eat at noontime, and he ain't no place in de room," she explained. "Dat cat musta got out someways."

"Oh, Aunt Phoebe, how am I ever going to find him?" Mandie said in exasperation. "Someone must have let him out, because we are always real careful to close the door when we leave."

"I figures he roamin' dis heah house somewhere," Aunt Phoebe said. "But I ain't seed him all day."

"If you do see him, would you please put him in our room and let me know?" Mandie asked. "I'll have to start looking and I suppose Celia will help me."

The two girls began searching the parlors and classrooms on the first floor. The other students had gone to their rooms or were walking outside. The workmen were working loudly in the basement.

After the girls finished searching the first floor without any luck, Mandie said, "Let's go ask the workmen if they've seen Snowball."

"You mean go in the basement where they're

making all that noise?" Celia asked as the two stopped in the front hallway.

"We've looked every place on this floor except Miss Prudence's and Miss Hope's private quarters, and I'm sure Miss Prudence would let me know if Snowball happened to ramble into her part of the house," Mandie replied. "We could just go down to the bottom of the cellar stairs and holler and ask the men if they've seen him."

"Well, all right, as long as you don't go any farther than that," Celia reluctantly agreed.

But when the two girls got to the cellar, the noise was so loud they couldn't make the men hear them. Mandie could see two of them banging on pipes farther into the basement. She quickly walked toward them while Celia stayed on the steps.

"Hello, have y'all seen my cat?" she called out, but the men still didn't seem to hear her.

As she stepped up behind them, she screamed with all her might, "Have y'all seen my cat?" But the men worked right on. She reached forward to pull on the sleeve of one of the men. He immediately turned around and looked at her in surprise. The other man also stopped work. "Have y'all seen my cat?" she asked again.

The two men frowned and looked at her and then at each other, without replying.

"I've lost my cat," Mandie explained. "Have you seen a white cat?"

The two men were plainly puzzled. They made signs to each other and then turned to look at Mandie as they motioned to indicate they could not hear.

"Oh, shucks!" Mandie murmured to herself as she made one last try. Puckering up her lips she tried to mouth the word "cat," but the men still stared without response. Mandie smiled at them, and they smiled back. She went back to join Celia on the steps.

"They're deaf, aren't they?" Celia asked.

"And I can't make them understand a thing," Mandie said with a sigh. "I don't suppose Snowball would be down here anyway, with all the noise those men make. Let's look out in the yard."

As they started up the steps, Mandie glanced back. The two men were still standing there, staring at her and Celia. She smiled and blew a kiss off her hand toward them. They smiled back and began quickly motioning to each other.

Luckily no one was around when the girls reached the top of the stairs leading into the back hallway from the basement. Mandie quietly closed the door as she said, "No wonder they make so much noise. They can't hear what they're doing."

The two girls stopped by the kitchen to check with Aunt Phoebe. The woman was sitting at the long table at the far end, drinking coffee. She shook her head as she informed them, "Ain't seed hide nor hair of dat white cat."

"We're going outside and look for him. Maybe he managed to sneak out of the house," Mandie told her.

"Mebbe," the woman said. "Y'all done look de whole house through?"

"We can't go into the other girls' rooms to look for him, but when we come back inside we'll go up to the attic and search it," Mandie told her.

"Dat attic s'posed to be kept shut all de time," Aunt Phoebe replied. "Doubt he got in dere. Most likely he be chasin' birds outside."

"We'll check with you later," Mandie promised as she and Celia left the kitchen.

When the girls went out into the backyard, they found Uncle Cal, Aunt Phoebe's husband, chopping wood. He stopped to talk to them.

"We're looking for Snowball, Uncle Cal. He has managed to get out of our room," Mandie told him.

"Don't believe I seed dat white cat all dis heah day. Most times Phoebe, she have him in de kitchen eatin' but not today dat I kin recollect," the old man replied as he rested his axe on the stump he was using for a chopping block.

"We'll look around, and if you see him, will you catch him and let me know?" Mandie asked. As she looked down and saw a box full of small tools, she asked, "Are you working on something with all those tools?"

"No, no, Missy, not right now," Uncle Cal said with a smile. "I been operatin' on de kitchen cabinet door whut wouldn't shut and jes' stopped heah to hit a lick or two on my way back to my house."

Mandie glanced toward the backyard where the tidy cottage that was Aunt Phoebe's and Uncle Cal's home stood. "Please let me know if you happen to see him," she told the old man.

"Dat I will, Missy, and I'll be sho' I ketch him, too," Uncle Cal said.

"Thanks," Mandie said as she and Celia walked on around the huge yard.

The two girls only saw four other students walking outside, but they were not friends, so they spoke and passed on around the schoolhouse to search the front yard. Finally giving up, Mandie and Celia went back inside the schoolhouse.

"Now what?" Celia asked as they stepped inside the front hallway.

"Let's go up to our room a minute to be sure he didn't somehow come back, and then we'll go on up to the attic," Mandie replied as she led the way up the front stairway.

But Snowball was still not in their room. Mandie sighed and said, "Well, on to the attic."

They climbed the narrow stairs to the door at the top. It was tightly shut.

"I don't see how Snowball could get in the attic with the door closed," Celia said as Mandie opened the door.

There was enough light coming in from the outside that the girls could see around the cluttered room. Boxes, trunks, old furniture, and other odds and ends were stacked from one end to the other, and there was barely room to move between.

"Someone could have opened the door here today, and Snowball could have slipped in without anyone seeing him. You know how nosey he is. He has to smell of everything," Mandie replied as they poked about the room. "Snowball! Here kitty, kitty!"

There was no response. As the girls stood there listening, only silence greeted them.

"Maybe if we could move some of these things, we could get in between all this stuff easier," Mandie said, bending to push a small trunk aside so she could step between it and a huge wardrobe.

"I'll help," Celia agreed.

The two moved about, pushing and shoving to clear a path. Then suddenly a box they were trying to move seemed stuck to the floor. They both put their weight behind it until it finally budged an inch or two.

"I don't know what's holding it," Mandie said, stooping to look down at the bottom of the box. "It doesn't seem to be all that heavy."

"It's like it's nailed to the floor or something," Celia said.

"Let's try again," Mandie said, standing up.

The two pushed with all their might, and the box finally began moving. Mandie looked down at the floor when the carton suddenly slid forward. "Look at what was holding it," Mandie said as she stooped down to investigate the boards of the floor. There was a huge nail sticking up that had worked its way out of one board. She pulled at the nail and found that the board was loose.

Celia joined her. "The floor is coming apart," she said as she watched Mandie.

Mandie lay down closer to the floor to peek through the crack caused by the loose board. "Celia, there's something under here," she said excitedly.

"I hope there's something under that board— something holding up the attic," Celia replied as she stooped to look.

"Come here, look," Mandie told her. She moved over a little to give Celia room to peek through the crack.

"Mandie, you're right," Celia said. "Looks like some old steps or something." She glanced at her friend in surprise.

"I know," Mandie agreed. "Let's see if we can get this board up."

The two girls pulled and pulled at the nail, but they couldn't get it out. It seemed to be in the board just far enough to keep the floor in place.

"I have an idea," Mandie said, sitting up suddenly. "Remember that toolbox Uncle Cal had in the backyard?"

"We'll just go borrow it," Celia added.

"Right," Mandie agreed as she stood up and brushed off her clothes.

At that moment the first bell for supper rang in the backyard. The two girls looked at each other in dismay.

"But we'll have to postpone borrowing that toolbox until after supper," Mandie told her friend.

"And we better go get cleaned up fast," Celia said as she looked down at her soiled dress.

The two girls quickly left the attic and hurried down the stairs to their room. They made their plans as they changed clothes.

"Just as soon as we are dismissed from the dining room, I'll go outside and see if Uncle Cal's toolbox is still there," Mandie told Celia.

"And what if it is gone?" Celia asked.

"Then we'll just find out where Uncle Cal keeps it," Mandie said.

"I hope we can find it without someone seeing us," Celia said.

"We'll find it," Mandie promised her.

The two rushed from their room and managed to be the last ones into the dining room.

Chapter 10 / Secret Doings

As soon as the evening meal was over, Mandie and Celia checked both their room and with Aunt Phoebe, but Snowball had not returned. They then walked out into the backyard with hopes of finding Uncle Cal's toolbox where they had seen it.

"Oh, shucks, it's gone," Mandie said in a disappointed voice as they approached the chopping block near which it had been sitting earlier.

"Uncle Cal is gone, too," Celia remarked. "I suppose he took it with him."

"But he was in the kitchen with Aunt Phoebe just now, and he didn't have the box with him," Mandie said.

She looked around the yard. "I wonder where he keeps it. I know he puts the rakes, and hoes, and shovels, and big tools like that under the end of his house. Let's see if he left the box there."

The two girls cautiously approached the cottage as they kept a lookout for any other students who might wander into the backyard. When they reached the side of the little house, they quickly stooped down to look under the end of the porch.

"I only see the big tools," Mandie said as she peered into the shadows underneath. She began moving some of them, but she didn't uncover the toolbox.

"I can't see any box, either," Celia agreed, stooping at Mandie's side.

Mandie stood up and brushed the dirt off her hands. "Well now, we'll have to do a little exploring."

As Mandie began circling the house, Celia followed. "What are you planning to do, Mandie? I hope no one sees us. Maybe we should at least wait until dark."

Mandie's eyes were busy searching the porches and the little outbuilding in the back.

"That building is not very big. Let's see if the door is unlocked," Mandie told Celia as she walked across the yard.

"Mandie, I feel like we are intruding on Uncle Cal's and Aunt Phoebe's private property," Celia protested as she reluctantly followed, glancing behind her.

But Mandie had already opened the door to the building. There, sitting in the corner, was the toolbox. "I've found it," she said, excitedly opening the lid. "Let's see. We need a claw hammer and a screwdriver, I think." She picked up the tools as she talked.

"And how are we going to get these tools up to the attic without someone seeing us?" Celia asked as she watched.

Mandie paused for a moment and then said, "I'll

hold the hammer under my skirt, like this." She pulled up her dress, positioned the hammer near her waistline, and carefully let her skirt back down while holding on to the tool through her dress. "And you take the screwdriver and do the same thing." She held out the screwdriver to Celia.

Celia slowly accepted it and tried to follow Mandie's instructions. After she had a grip on the tool through her skirt, she said, "You know, this could be dangerous. What if we drop these things?"

"Oh, Celia, stop worrying," Mandie told her as she carefully closed the toolbox. "We'll go up the back stairs, which come out near our room and which the other students don't ever use. And since our room is near the attic steps, no one will see us. Come on."

Mandie walked back across the yard, carefully holding the hammer under her skirt, and Celia stayed close behind her. When they were finally on the steps, Celia said, "I don't know why we couldn't have just asked Uncle Cal to borrow his hammer and screwdriver instead of sneaking around like this."

Mandie answered in a low voice as they quietly came out into the hallway near their room, "Because that would get Uncle Cal involved in this, and I don't want someone else to get in trouble because of me."

"Well, thanks a lot," Celia replied. "I'm in this with you."

Mandie quietly led the way up the steps to the attic. There was a kerosene lamp kept by the door and matches to light it, but Mandie could see with the daylight through the windows, so she didn't bother with the lamp. She found the place in the floor they had discovered earlier.

"I don't think this will make much noise," Mandie said as she took the claw hammer and began pulling at the nail in the board. "This thing sure is tough."

Celia watched. She held out the screwdriver and asked, "Why don't you wedge this between the boards?"

"Good idea," Mandie agreed as she took the screwdriver and managed to insert the end of it between the loose boards. Then she struck it hard with the hammer, and the plank suddenly flew up. "We're making progress." She peeked through the hole in the floor. "It is a staircase going down under here. I wonder where it goes."

Celia bent to look. "Well, I wonder why someone put a floor over it," she said.

"We'll find out," Mandie said as she continued working on the loose boards in the floor.

Finally they had removed enough of the boards to make room for them to go through.

Mandie stooped to look down. "It's dark down there," she said.

"Are you going down there, Mandie?" Celia asked as she gazed into the space below.

Mandie stood up and said, "I think we'd better get a candle and some matches. You wait here. I'll run back down to our room to get them."

Celia didn't say anything, but as Mandie hurried out the attic door, she went to stand on the landing outside until Mandie returned, armed with a pocketful of matches and two large candles.

"You one, me one," Mandie told her as she handed a candle and matches to Celia. "Come on."

Celia accepted them and followed Mandie back

across the attic to the hole revealing the steps. The girls lit their candles. Then Celia stopped and stubbornly asked, "Mandie, why are you so interested in going down there? I don't think I want to go."

Mandie looked at her as she put out her foot and tested the first step. It seemed stout enough to hold her weight. "Celia, if you don't want to go, stay here, but I'm going to see what's down there." She held her candle above her head and slowly stepped down onto the next step.

"All right," Celia finally agreed as she followed. "But don't say I didn't warn you if we run into rats and spiders down there." She stayed close behind Mandie and held on to her lighted candle.

The candles cast eery shadows on the steps, and it was impossible to see anything but the stairs. Mandie carefully stepped down from one step to the next. Suddenly they came to a large landing. Mandie held her candle up to inspect it.

"Look! There's a door!" Mandie exclaimed as she tried to open it. The door wouldn't budge. "Must be locked," she said.

Celia frowned as she bent to look. "No, it's not, Mandie," she said. "There's no lock on it, just that catch on this side."

"You're right," Mandie agreed as she tried releasing the rusted hook. "Hold this a minute, please." She handed Celia her candle and worked on the door. Finally it gave way, and she was able to pull the door open. The girls were astonished to be greeted by a blank wall behind the door. "Well, of all things!"

"Can we go back now, Mandie?" Celia asked as Mandie took her candle back.

"No, we haven't found out where the steps go

yet. We'll just leave that door for later,'' Mandie told her as she turned to continue down the steps from the landing.

As she walked down, Mandie tried to figure out which floors they passed. Then a musty odor met her nostrils, and she realized they were going into the basement below the house. She looked down what seemed to be the last flight and could vaguely see what must be a small air vent with a dim light coming through.

''This is the last flight,'' Mandie said, glancing back at Celia, who was close behind her.

''Where are we?'' Celia asked in a frightened voice.

''The basement—'' Mandie started to say when suddenly the staircase gave way. She and Celia fell into the area below.

''Oh!'' Celia cried as she scrambled to find her candle, which had gone out.

''Are you all right?'' Mandie asked as she got up from the floor and took a match from her pocket and relit her candle. She glanced overhead. The staircase had broken away, and a piece of it was hanging over their heads.

Celia found her candle and touched the wick to Mandie's. ''Mandie, how are we ever going to get out of here?'' she asked, almost in tears as she, too, looked up at the broken steps.

Suddenly there was a loud meow. Mandie quickly looked around. She could see by the light of her candle that they were in a section of the basement she had never seen, but somewhere around here she was sure she'd find Snowball.

''Snowball, where are you?'' Mandie called loudly.

"Up there, Mandie," Celia said, pointing overhead.

The white cat was clinging to a piece of the rotten wooden steps and began meowing loudly without stopping.

"Snowball, I don't know how you think we're going to get you down," Mandie said, backing away against a wall to look up at him.

Then there was a scuttling noise, and Mandie glimpsed a large rat out of the corner of her eye. Celia also saw it and the two girls clung to each other in fright.

Snowball made a jump down from his perch in an effort to catch the rat. The girls watched as the rat seemed to go into the brick wall. Snowball began clawing at the bricks.

"Too late, Snowball. He's gone," Mandie told the cat as she drew a deep breath.

But Snowball seemed to know better. He kept digging at the wall and managed to get a brick loose enough to fall out.

"Celia, look!" Mandie told her friend as she bent over to look through the hole in the brick wall. "I do believe there's another wall or something behind this." She started pulling at another loose brick. Celia came up behind her and helped.

"If only we had that screwdriver and hammer we left in the attic," Celia said as the girls broke their fingernails on the rough wall while they held the candles in their other hands.

"Watch out, another brick is coming out," Mandie told Celia as she jerked hard on one of the bricks in the wall. It tumbled out and landed on the floor. Mandie looked closely at the space they had uncovered, and she became excited. "Celia, there's another door behind this. Look!" She pointed to a rusted hinge behind the brick.

Celia quickly looked where Mandie was pointing and said, "I don't understand why someone went around sealing up doors and steps in this house."

"I wonder what is on the other side," Mandie said, quickly digging away at the bricks which now seemed to fall away more easily.

As soon as they had made a hole large enough to push on the old door, the girls stuck their burning candles on bricks nearby and began trying to open the door. All this time Snowball had sat quietly watching. He was afraid of fire, so he moved back a little distance from the candles.

After a lot of pushing and banging, the old door gave way a couple of inches, and the two girls together managed to move it enough to force their way through the crack.

"It's dark in here! The candles!" Mandie exclaimed as she reached through the opening of the door to retrieve the candles.

The room they found themselves in was long and narrow. The first thing Mandie noticed was some kind of writing on the wall directly in front of them.

"Look at this," Mandie said as she held up her candle to inspect it. "Why, it's a riddle." She read on:

" 'Turn to your left and then about face,
Two steps forward, then back one pace.

Look o'er your head, down at your feet.
Now cross your eyes and stand up neat.

Turn round and round and count to four.
Look really hard and you will find the door.' "

She looked puzzled. "But we've already found the door."

"I hope there's another door out of here, because the stairs are gone, and we can't go back out that way," Celia said worriedly.

"Let's try this silly riddle, just for fun. You read it for me, and I'll do what it says," Mandie told her.

Celia repeated the riddle, and Mandie acted it out. At the end she looked around and didn't see any other door. "I'll read it, and you do it," Mandie told her friend.

As Mandie read the writing, Celia followed the commands but without any more luck than Mandie had. "Whoever wrote it must have meant the door we just came through," Celia decided.

Mandie held her candle up and moved about the room. "This must be some kind of storage room," she said. "Look at all those trunks and boxes." She moved closer to inspect them.

"They sure are old," Celia commented as she followed.

Snowball had followed them into the room and was roaming around, smelling everything. He made a sudden lunge at a rat that had jumped up on the top of an old trunk. The girls watched as the rat instantly disappeared through a hole in the trunk lid. The cat began pawing through the hole.

"Mandie, we need to find a way out of here," Celia reminded her friend, who had stepped closer to watch the cat.

"Celia, there's jewelry or something inside that trunk. See Snowball pulling at a strand of something through the hole," Mandie told her as they watched.

"Well, I'm not about to open it," Celia said, shivering.

"If I had something to poke it with . . ." Mandie said, trying to see what else was in the room. Her eyes went back to the door they had come through. A piece of wood was hanging from the side of it. She rushed over to pull at it.

Celia came to help, and they managed to free it from the door.

"I'll try this," Mandie said, swinging it in the air. "Watch out for the rat that went inside that trunk." She looked at Snowball, who was still sitting on top. "Snowball, you grab it quick if it comes out. Here goes." She stuck the stick out and punched at the hole in the lid. Nothing happened, but the cat stayed on guard.

"Mandie, don't get too close," Celia warned her as she watched.

Mandie managed to get the stick through a loop in the strand hanging out through the hole. She pulled, and it came out. She pulled it near her and then bent to inspect what she had found. "It is some kind of jewelry, but it looks old. I believe it's a necklace."

Celia quickly joined Mandie, stooping to inspect the strand. By the light of the two candles the girls decided it was an old necklace encrusted with dirt. There seemed to be some kind of jewels set here and there along the strand, and metal strings hung on the edge like a fringe.

Then a sudden thought dawned on Mandie. "There may be more jewelry in that trunk!" she exclaimed as she stood up and walked over to it.

"The rat, Mandie," Celia warned her.

But at that moment the rat jumped from another

hole in the trunk. Snowball chased after it and captured it in the corner of the room.

"He got it," Mandie said as she continued toward the trunk. Celia slowly followed.

Together the two girls managed to raise the lid, which fell to pieces as they pushed it open. They gaped in wonder as the light of their candles revealed a trunk crammed full of jewelry, old and dirty with age. They both reached inside to explore.

"This is so old it stinks," Mandie said as she wrinkled her nose at the musty scent. She held up another necklace with two fingers.

"It's probably over a hundred years old, Mandie," Celia remarked as she lifted out a wide, jeweled bracelet.

Mandie looked at her and asked, "How do you know?"

"Remember all the museums we visited in Europe and all the old artifacts—jewelry, clothes, and other things we saw? This stuff looks every bit as old as what we saw over there," Celia explained. "And these things are probably real."

"You mean real jewels, real gold?" Mandie asked as she continued poking inside the trunk.

"Yes, real in every way," Celia told her. She glanced at the candle in one hand. "Mandie, my candle is burning down. We need to get out of here before we get left in the dark for good."

Mandie looked at her candle. "I know we'd better get out," she said, "but how?" She straightened up to look around the room. At the far end of the long narrow place, she noticed there was something standing up larger than the trunks and boxes stacked here and there. Quickly walking down that way, she discovered there were stacks of paintings leaning against the wall. "Look, Celia! Artwork!"

Celia followed her and said, "These look very old, too."

Mandie started flipping trunk lids here and there, wherever she could find one that would open. Inside every trunk and box she found old treasures. "We must have found a fortune."

"A huge fortune," Celia agreed.

"If we can find a way out of here we can come back and look at everything later," Mandie said. "Evidently no one knows this is all here."

"Let's say our verse, Mandie, and I'll feel better," Celia said.

Mandie reached for her hand, and together they said their favorite verse, "What time I am afraid, I will put my trust in Thee." The girls squeezed each other's hands.

"Now let's try the riddle again. There must be some solution to it," Mandie said.

They didn't figure out the answer to the riddle, but each time they tried it, they ended up facing the same wall, so Mandie decided it was time to explore that wall. The bricks were much looser than those that had been in the other wall.

The girls once again began digging loose bricks from the wall. After more broken fingernails, they found another door behind the brick.

"Oh look, this door moves," Mandie said, excitedly pushing on it after they had uncovered a large place in the wall. It swung open, and they found themselves in the section of the basement where the workmen had been installing the furnace.

Mandie reached down and picked up Snowball, who had been following them. "You don't run away again, mister," she told him as she held him with one arm while she had the candle in her other hand. He meowed his reply. She shut the old door behind them. "I think I see the steps ahead where we came down to speak to the workmen."

"At last," Celia said with a big sigh as they reached the top of the basement stairs. They paused to listen and silently, slowly opened the door to the hallway. Everything was quiet. They blew out their candles and were able to get up the back staircase without being seen by anyone.

Mandie pushed open the door to their room and entered. Celia came in quickly and closed it behind them. Mandie dropped Snowball to the floor, and the two girls collapsed into chairs.

Mandie looked at Celia's dirty clothes, and Celia looked at Mandie's filthy garments, then both girls burst into uncontrollable giggles.

In the middle of this, there was a light tap on their door. They both straightened up and looked at each other.

"Come in," Mandie called with a worried expression. She was concerned about being caught by anyone in this condition.

Aunt Phoebe stuck her head inside the doorway and said, "Just checkin' to see if dat white cat been found." She looked from one girl to the other but didn't remark on their appearances.

"Oh yes, Aunt Phoebe, just now," Mandie told her. "He was in the basement. That's where we got so dirty." She stood up.

"Den whilst y'all git cleaned up, I git dat cat sumpin' to eat and bring it up heah. Best he don't go out agin tonight," she told Mandie. "Be right back."

"Thank goodness that was Aunt Phoebe and not

somebody else," Mandie said with a sigh of relief. "Let's make ourselves decent." She laughed as she looked down at her soiled dress. Celia stood up and twirled around in hers.

Mandie looked at the clock and realized it would be time to go to bed by the time they were cleaned up. She wondered where the evening had gone.

Aunt Phoebe returned with a plate heaped full of delicious scraps for Snowball and fresh water for his water bowl by his sandbox in the corner. Mandie could tell she was curious about where they had been, but she didn't ask any questions, and Mandie didn't volunteer any information. She didn't want to get her involved in anything that could cause trouble.

After they were in bed for the night, the two girls talked a long time about their discovery and what they should do about it.

"I think we should tell Miss Prudence about what we found," Celia suggested.

"Not Miss Prudence," Mandie objected. "Why not tell my grandmother? She owns the school building now anyway." She pushed up on her pillow.

"All right, we'll tell her," Celia agreed as she sat up beside her in the bed.

"But not right away. We have to have time to look through everything first, so we'll know what we're talking about," Mandie said. "And, Celia, I just remembered something. We left the floor torn up in the attic. And we left Uncle Cal's hammer and screwdriver up there, too. We need to get up there real early in the morning, and place things back like they were, and return his tools before he misses them."

"And when do you plan on going back down to that room in the basement? Even though we closed the door behind us, those workmen might notice that the door has been opened, and since they're working every day until suppertime, that means they'd see us go in there unless we wait until after they finish for the day," Celia said.

"We'll just have to wait for them to leave tomorrow night, because we won't have time before classes in the morning. Besides, we'll probably get all dirty again," Mandie told her. Snowball stood up on the foot of the bed, walked around in circles, then lay back down. "Snowball started all this. I wonder how he got down there anyway."

"He must have found a secret way," Celia said with a laugh.

Suddenly Mandie remembered the rug being pushed off the hole in the floor when they came into the room earlier that day. "The rug, Celia!" she exclaimed. "Snowball had evidently pushed the rug off the hole the workmen made in our floor. Do you suppose he managed to get down through that hole and on into the basement?"

"Oh, Mandie, that's exactly what he must have done, and it was so dark down there we couldn't see any hole that he came through," Celia agreed.

"Well, we'd better put something heavy on that rug when we leave the room tomorrow so he can't do it again," Mandie said. She moved around on her pillow as she plumped it up. "I'd just like to know why those steps were sealed off and where all the stuff in that room came from."

"We may never know," Celia said as she slipped down in the bed and put her head on her pillow.

"Celia Hamilton, are you daring me? You know

I'll never let this go unsolved," Mandie said with a big smile as she lay back down.

"This mystery is too old, Mandie," Celia told her.

"Old, but never *too* old," Mandie murmured as she let sleep close her eyes.

She dreamed about the door on the landing of the secret stairs that opened into a blank wall. In her dream she opened it and found Celia standing on the other side.

Chapter 11 / Past Secrets

Roosters crowing in the backyard woke Mandie the next morning. She nudged Celia and jumped out of bed.

"The attic," Mandie reminded her friend as she quickly put on a dress.

"Oh me!" Celia groaned as she yawned and slid out onto the carpet. "Let's just get this over with."

The two girls hurried up to the attic after they had dressed, and they soon had the floorboards back in place and the trunk back over it.

Mandie picked up Uncle Cal's hammer and screwdriver and said, "Now we have to return these." She handed Celia the screwdriver as she hid the hammer in the folds of her dress.

They crept down the back stairs, hoping no one was in the kitchen yet. There was complete silence, but when they opened the back door and stepped outside, they came face-to-face with Uncle Cal and

Aunt Phoebe, who were coming to prepare breakfast.

"You girls sure are up and out awfully early," the old woman said.

Before they could answer, Uncle Cal grinned and said, "And I know why." He held out his hand as he added, "If y'all will jes' give me dat hammer and screwdriver, I'll jes' put 'em back in de box."

Mandie and Celia looked at each other in shock, then silently held out the tools they were carrying.

"But, Uncle Cal, how did you know we had them?" Mandie asked.

"I come out de do' to git mo' wood fo' de stove last night, and I seed y'all standin' in de do'way of de shed wid de tools. But don't y'all worry none. Y'all musta had a good reason to borrow dem," the old man said as he took the tools.

"Whut y'all been up to now?" Aunt Phoebe asked.

Mandie and Celia looked at each other again, and then Mandie said, "Oh well, I know y'all never give away our secrets, so I'll just tell you. We found some loose planks in the attic floor, and when we pulled them up we found some secret steps."

"Secret steps under de flo' in de attic?" the old woman asked with a gasp.

"Y'all ain't kiddin' us ole folks, are you?" Uncle Cal asked.

"No, we really did find some old rotten steps that go down into the basement, and we're going to tell my grandmother about it after we do a little investigating, so please don't tell on us."

"Lawsy mercy, whut kinda house we be livin' in?" Aunt Phoebe asked in astonishment.

"We'll show y'all later if you want to see," Celia spoke up.

"We sho' do," Uncle Cal said. "But right now we gotta git dat breakfus' ready fo' all dem young ladies."

Mandie and Celia turned back and ran into the house and up the back stairway to their room.

The two girls couldn't keep their minds on their lessons that day. They were wishing for the day to end so they could return to the basement to go through the treasures they had found.

But Mrs. Taft came to the school as their last class was being dismissed for the day. She was going to the courthouse to record the deed to the school building, which she had recently bought from Miss Prudence and her sister, Miss Hope, and wanted to take Mandie with her to show how it was done.

"You need to begin learning about the business world, Amanda," Mrs. Taft told her after Miss Prudence had given permission and as Ben was driving them to the courthouse for Buncombe County in downtown Asheville. Celia had also been allowed to go with them. "I'm sure you'll have some property transfers to do sometime. This is a good time to start."

Mandie looked at her and said, "Yes, ma'am."

"I've been to the courthouse at home with my mother," Celia told them.

Once inside the courthouse, Mrs. Taft led the way to the office of the Registrar of Deeds. As they entered the room, Mandie and Celia looked around at the dozens and dozens of huge books stacked on shelves all the way around the room. A middle-aged lady with spectacles and her gray hair pinned on top of her head was sitting at a desk near the door.

Mrs. Taft approached her and said as she held out the deed, "I would like to record this, and I brought my granddaughter and her friend along to watch."

"Yes, ma'am," the lady said as she accepted the paper and carefully read it over. "Everything seems to be in order. Now for the fees." She consulted a book on the desk.

Mrs. Taft paid the fees. The woman stamped the document, recorded it in her huge book, and handed it back to Mrs. Taft who then walked over to the shelves.

The girls watched and listened.

"Now, if you want to look up someone's name and see what property they own, you first look in the index for the name. There are two books, one for the grantee and one for the grantor, that is, the buyer and the seller. In other words, you are able to look up my name and find out the names of people I have purchased property from all the way back. And you would be able to find any property willed or given to someone also. And you can keep going back and find out who that person received the property from." She paused and looked at them.

"Sort of like a family history? Your property would be recorded here, and your parents' before that, and their parents' before that, and so on?" Mandie questioned.

Mrs. Taft smiled and said, "In a way it's a genealogy of property."

Another lady had entered the room and was listening to Mrs. Taft's conversation. When she paused, the tall lady smiled and asked, "And how are you today, Mrs. Taft?" Her teeth were sparkling white even though her face showed signs of wear.

"Just fine, Miss Hamby," Mrs. Taft replied, also with a smile. "I'd like you to meet my granddaughter, Amanda, and her friend Celia Hamilton."

"Elizabeth's daughter," Miss Hamby replied as she looked at Mandie. "The spittin' image of her mother, isn't she?" Her brown eyes crinkled as she smiled.

Mandie felt uncomfortable at the appraisal and said, "Oh, but my mother isn't part Cherokee like I am."

"Why, that's right, you are," Miss Hamby replied. "I am a genealogist, and I've traced quite a few people's ancestry in this town, and I remember that your father was half Cherokee."

"Yes, ma'am," Mandie agreed.

"We must go now, girls. Y'all probably have homework to do," Mrs. Taft said, starting for the door. "Good day, Miss Hamby."

As Miss Hamby bid them goodbye, Mandie glanced back to look at her again. She seemed to be an awfully interesting person due to the fact that she traced other people's ancestors.

The girls had homework—lots of it—that day. They were nowhere finished when the bell rang for supper, and Mandie knew they would never be able to go down to the basement after the evening meal. They would do well to complete their studies by the time the bell rang for curfew at ten o'clock.

"Whew!" Mandie said, laying down her pencil and notebook as she finally finished. Looking at the clock on the bureau, she said, "Almost bedtime. Why do all the teachers give us so much to do at one time?"

Celia closed her book and stretched. She

laughed and said, "They're probably all in cahoots together to keep us from doing anything else."

"Like going back down to that secret room in the basement," Mandie said with a big sigh. "Maybe tomorrow night we can go." She stood up, picked up her pillow from the bed, and squeezed it tight. "I think we need some exercise, like a good pillow fight, maybe?" She grinned at her friend.

"I'm all for it," Celia agreed. "Just let me get my shoes and dress off."

Mandie removed hers also and the two girls jumped up on the bed and began batting the pillows back and forth at each other.

"I know we're too old for this, but it's fun," Mandie said as she slammed Celia with her pillow.

Celia fought back, and the game got fast and furious. Suddenly, before the girls knew what had happened, the bed fell in and threw them down with it.

"Oh, oh. We're in trouble," Mandie said as she scrambled to her feet and stepped onto the floor.

Celia followed. "Where is Snowball? Did he get caught beneath the bed?" she asked.

Mandie hurriedly searched the room and found her white cat with his fur ruffled up, sitting in a far corner. "No, he had sense enough to get out of the way," she said. She turned back to look at the bed. The mattress was lying on the floor, and the bedstead stood at a crooked angle. Then her eyes noticed the wall behind the head of the bed. She ran to see what had happened.

"Celia, look! The head of the bed knocked a hole in the wall, all the way through the plaster. What are we going to do?" Mandie exclaimed as she surveyed the damage.

"I don't know, Mandie," Celia said with a gasp.

Mandie moved closer to the hole in the wall. "I wonder where this hole goes through to," she said, trying to get all the way to the damaged place. "There isn't another room next to us, remember? This is the end of the hallway." She stepped up on the fallen mattress to put her eye next to the hole. "I can't see anything. It's dark in there."

Celia ran for the lamp. "Here, I'll hold the lamp up while you look," she said.

Mandie looked again. "There's something inside the wall," she exclaimed. "Looks like papers." She turned to look around the room. "I need something to pry it out. Will you hand me the shoehorn off the bureau?"

Celia quickly got the shoehorn and gave it to her. Mandie began poking at the hole in the plaster, and it gradually grew a little larger. She could definitely see something inside.

"Can you get it out?" Celia asked as she continued to hold the lamp up.

Finally the hole was large enough for Mandie to put her hand inside, and she pulled at the object. She twisted and turned it and pulled with all her might. It suddenly came out, and Mandie lost her balance and fell back onto the mattress.

Celia set the lamp down on the table and hurried to look. "What is it, Mandie?"

"I'm not sure," Mandie said as she sat up on the mattress and looked at an old book in her hand. "It's a book and it's awfully old. In fact it's almost crumbling up."

The two girls bent over the book and slowly deciphered the ancient handwriting inside.

"Why, it's a diary or something," Mandie exclaimed as she scanned the pages.

Celia by her side kept reading. "Mandie, this says, *Set sail at first light this twenty-fourth of June in the year of 1789. Ships carrying valuable cargo travel this time of day. And we did encounter one such ship. They were armed but we managed to board it and take what we wanted, beautiful jeweled gowns headed for the New World.*" She stopped to gasp.

Mandie felt a thrill run over her body. "Pirates! Pirates, Celia!" she exclaimed, and then she stopped to think. "But how did this diary get in this house?"

"I think you call it a ship's log," Celia corrected her. "The pirate must have lived here, or something."

Mandie grasped Celia's hand and squeezed it hard. "You're right. That stuff in the cellar must have belonged to a pirate, a real pirate, who lived right here in this house!"

"Oh, Mandie, what are we going to do?" Celia asked worriedly.

Mandie stood up and stepped over to lay the book on the bureau. "First of all, we'd better get this bed put back together. I sure hope no one heard the noise," she said as she began pulling off the tangled bedcovers.

Celia helped, and together they managed to stand the bed back up; but it was hard work trying to get the slats spaced under the heavy mattress so it wouldn't fall in again. Finally they stood back and surveyed their work.

"It's all fixed now except for the hole in the wall," Mandie said as she looked at the spot where the bed had broken the plaster.

"Someone will see that for sure," Celia said.

"You know what I think?" Mandie asked as she went back to peep into the hole. "I believe that door that we found on the landing opened into this room at one time, and this hole here is in the wall behind the door." She looked at Celia.

Celia came to look inside, too. "I think you're right, Mandie. That would make sense because we couldn't get through that door, and it was just about this level in the house," she agreed.

"Well, I don't think I want to go back to see," Mandie said as she walked about the room. "We've already stopped up the floor in the attic, and the se-cret stairway collapsed in the basement, so we can't come up from there." She thought for a mo-ment. "I know what we can do about the hole, though. If we push the bed over far enough, the headboard will cover the hole."

"Yes, but what about rats with that hole right be-hind our heads at night?" Celia asked.

"Snowball will watch out for us, and tomorrow we can tack something over the hole," Mandie told her. "Let's get ready for bed so we can finish read-ing this pirate's log."

When they were ready, they propped up on their pillows and after reading about several ships being looted, the girls came to a part where the man had reformed.

"God, please forgive me. My daughter died be-cause of my sins. I have nothing left. I've put all I had taken from that missionary ship into the room in the cellar where my darling daughter used to write on the walls—bless her little soul—because I do not know how to return it to its rightful owners. I have sealed up the contents of my sins and will

place this where no one will find it. Satan, get thee behind me." It was signed *"Jeremiah Grey, lately of Charles Town, South Carolina."* And that was the end of the log.

"Grey!" Mandie said with a loud gasp. "Remember Etrulia said Tommy Patton had an ancestor named Grey who was a pirate, and then April Snow said she had one named Grey, too. You don't suppose . . ." She stopped as she assembled her thoughts.

"That this man was one of their ancestors?" Celia finished for her.

"Yes, this man evidently lived in Charleston, which was Charles Town then, sometime or other," Mandie said as she continued trying to sort out the story.

At that moment, the curfew bell rang. Mandie jumped out of bed. She raised the long scarf on the bureau and put the log beneath it.

"I've got to wash my hands," she said.

"Me too," Celia added.

Finally back in bed, the girls discussed their discoveries.

"We've just got to find out who this man was and where all that stuff came from," Mandie said as she bunched up her pillow.

"He says he stole it from a missionary ship, Mandie," Celia reminded her.

"But what missionary ship? How could we find out who the owners were?" Mandie puzzled.

"Maybe your grandmother could help us sort this all out," Celia suggested.

"Maybe, but I have an idea," Mandie told her. "First let's see if we can find that Miss Hamby who traces ancestors and ask her if she ever knew of anyone named Grey."

"All right, but there are probably dozens of people named Grey," Celia reminded her.

"But that long ago—the log was written over a hundred years ago," Mandie reminded her. "There probably wouldn't have been so many people living here in Asheville and, therefore, probably not many by the name of Grey."

"How are we going to find Miss Hamby?" Celia asked.

"Grandmother would know where she lives, but come to think of it, Miss Prudence probably knows where to find her since everybody knows everybody in this town," Mandie replied. "I'll ask Miss Prudence."

And the next morning when the girls were dismissed from breakfast, Mandie waited outside the dining room door for Miss Prudence to come out. She stepped up to the headmistress as she started down the hallway.

"Miss Prudence, could I just ask you if you happen to know Miss Hamby who traces people's ancestors?" Mandie quickly asked.

The headmistress paused to look at her and said, "Why, of course, everyone in town knows her—and, I might add, she knows everyone in town and their ancestors, too."

"Would you know where she lives, where to find her? We met her at the courthouse with my grandmother," Mandie told her.

"Miss Hamby lives in that big white house down on the next corner, the one with the green shutters and the green rockers on the porch," Miss Prudence replied as she looked at Mandie curiously.

"Would you give Celia and me permission to visit her after classes this afternoon? Just for a little while?" Mandie asked, eagerly waiting for her response.

"Well, I suppose so, but mind you now, you will have to let me or Miss Hope know when you go and come," Miss Prudence agreed. "I have to hurry now." She went on down the hallway.

Mandie and Celia looked at each other in glee. "We're going to see Miss Hamby," they chimed together as they raced up the stairs to get their books to begin classes for the day.

And the minute their last class for the day was over, they rushed back to their room, threw their books inside, checked to be sure Snowball was still there and that he hadn't moved the rugs out of place, and raced back downstairs. They found Miss Hope in her office.

"Miss Prudence gave us permission to go see Miss Hamby," Mandie told her.

"Yes, my sister told me," Miss Hope said. "Are y'all planning to trace your ancestors?"

"Oh no, not ours," Mandie said. "You see, she's a friend of my grandmother, and we just wanted—"

"You don't have to explain to me, Amanda," Miss Hope interrupted with a smile. "My sister gave you permission, so run along, and be sure to let me know when you return."

"Thanks," Mandie said.

As they started to leave, Miss Hope said, "Oh, wait a minute. Celia, you are on the music schedule to go study with Miss Marston at Mrs. Taft's house for a lesson tonight and, Amanda, you are on for tomorrow night. Of course, both of these lessons will be after suppertime. I just wanted to remind you."

"Thanks," Mandie said with a slight groan as she and Celia left the office and went down the hallway.

"I'm glad I'm beginning my lessons," Celia remarked as they got to the front door.

"But you know what that means," Mandie reminded her. "You will be tied up tonight, and I will be tomorrow night, and we won't be able to get back down in the cellar either night."

"Well," Celia said thoughtfully. "Sooner or later we'll make it."

The two girls walked down the roadway and found the house Miss Prudence had described. As they went up the long walkway, Mandie tried to see inside the floor-length windows on the front of the house, but long curtains blinded her view.

Once on the porch, Mandie took a deep breath and knocked with the round brass knocker on the big front door. She could hear it echo inside. The house must be enormous, she thought.

The door opened almost immediately, and Miss Hamby stood there looking at the girls in surprise, and then she stepped back and motioned them inside.

"Come in. Do come in. The parlor is over here," she told them as she led the way and waved her hand toward seats. "This is a nice surprise."

"We won't take up much of your time, Miss Hamby. We just wanted to ask you a question," Mandie began, suddenly realizing she didn't know how to inquire about the pirate as she and Celia sat on the settee.

"Of course, what can I do for you young ladies?" Miss Hamby asked as she sat down on a chair nearby.

"You said you could trace ancestors," Mandie began. "Can you trace people all the way back to 1789?"

Miss Hamby looked at her in surprise. "Why, probably," she said. "I've done lots of research further back than that on certain families. Who is it you wish to know about, dear?"

"A man named Jeremiah Grey, and he used to live in Charleston, but in 1789 he was living here in Asheville," Mandie told her.

"Is this man a relative of yours?" Miss Hamby asked.

"Oh no, never," Mandie quickly replied.

"Then, you are doing this for someone else?" the lady asked.

"No, well, you see, we found his name in . . . a book, and we'd just like to know something about him," Mandie replied.

"In a book? Could I see the book, just to see what it said about him?" Miss Hamby asked.

Mandie was beginning to be sorry she had come. "Well, you see, the book doesn't belong to me and—" she paused.

"And we don't have the book right now," Celia added.

Mandie looked at her friend and realized she was not telling a lie because they didn't have the ship's log with them right at that time.

"Well, that's all right, then. Now let me write this down," Miss Hamby said, getting up to walk over to a desk by the window. She picked up a notebook and a pencil and wrote in it. "Jeremiah Grey—do you know whether that's spelled with an 'e' or with an 'a'?" she asked.

"Oh, with an 'e.' It's G-R-E-Y," Mandie spelled the name out for her.

"I'll look into it for you, but right now I have an appointment and must get ready to go out," the lady told them.

The girls stood up and followed her as she started for the hallway. At the front door Mandie asked, "Do you have any idea how long this will take?"

"I just never know," Miss Hamby said. "Sometimes I'm lucky, and sometimes I never seem to accomplish much. But I'll let you know."

As they stepped out onto the front porch, Mandie asked, "Would you mind if we check back with you? You see, we don't want everyone at school knowing what we're doing."

"Aha!" Miss Hamby said with a smile. "Of course you girls come back whenever you like. You're welcome anytime."

"Thank you, Miss Hamby," Mandie said.

"And I thank you, too, Miss Hamby," Celia added as they started down the long walkway. Miss Hamby waved to them and closed the front door.

As soon as they had walked to the roadway, Mandie blew out her breath and said, "I had no idea she would ask so many questions."

"Remember Miss Prudence said she knows all about everyone in town, so she is probably wondering who this Jeremiah Grey was, whether he was connected to your grandmother's family or not," Celia reminded her as they walked along.

"I have no idea about when to go back to see if she has found out anything," Mandie said.

"We can just guess. And she did say we were welcome anytime," Celia said.

The girls checked back in with Miss Hope when they returned to the school and then went upstairs to read the log again while they waited for the supper bell.

Chapter 12 / Sorting It All Out!

Celia had her music lesson that night, and Mandie went for hers the next night, Thursday. She couldn't make her mind up whether she was going to enjoy the lessons or not.

On Friday, Mrs. Taft came to take Mandie and Celia to her house for the weekend. Therefore, the girls still had not had a chance to return to the cellar to examine the treasures they had found. And they had not seen Miss Hamby.

But the puzzle began unraveling on Sunday at church. As the congregation was leaving, Mandie and Celia stepped outside the front door with Mrs. Taft and they found Miss Hamby waiting for them on the porch.

"I found such interesting information about Jeremiah Grey, I thought I'd take a moment to tell you," Miss Hamby began as she spoke to Mrs. Taft and then to the girls.

"Jeremiah Grey?" Mrs. Taft asked.

"Yes, you see he was a notorious pirate, and he was born here in Asheville but shipped out of Charles Town, South Carolina," Miss Hamby quickly went on. "I found some old newspaper reports on his daughter, how she was murdered by someone trying to steal his treasures. Of course the law never found whoever did it, but Jeremiah Grey made a complete turnabout, quit the sea, and shut himself up in that house you use for a schoolhouse now. He was found dead one day in the backyard by a traveling peddler. Apparently he had had some health problems. That was in 1820, I believe—"

Mrs. Taft spoke loudly as she interrupted, "Just a moment if you please, Miss Hamby. Who in the world are you talking about? Why are you telling us this?"

Miss Hamby immediately looked at the girls. They both avoided her gaze as Mandie said, "We asked Miss Hamby to get us some information on this man. We found his name in a book at school."

"Well, why didn't someone say so in the first place?" Mrs. Taft asked.

"I'm sorry, Mrs. Taft," Miss Hamby said. "I thought you were aware that the girls had asked me to do this." Looking at Mandie, she added, "I'll bring you my report, and Mrs. Taft the bill, then."

"Bill?" Mandie gasped as she realized Miss Hamby was in the business of finding information and expected to be paid.

"An itemized bill, if you please, Miss Hamby," Mrs. Taft replied. "Now, girls, let's go on home."

"Yes, Mrs. Taft, I will be happy to," Miss Hamby called after them.

As soon as they were all in Mrs. Taft's rig and on the way to her house, Mandie told her, "I'm sorry,

Grandmother, but I couldn't explain to you in front of Miss Hamby because we have come across a deep, dark secret and I didn't want to share it with Miss Hamby. But you see, we found a ship's log with this Jeremiah Grey's name on it." She paused.

"All right, dear, I'll pay her fee. If it's for school, I don't mind," Mrs. Taft said as Ben, her driver, cut a corner sharply.

"But it's not exactly for school, at least not for school lessons," Mandie said as she kept her balance on the seat. "And not only that, we found all kinds of treasures in a secret room in the cellar at school—"

That caught Mrs. Taft's attention immediately. "Amanda, will you please begin at the beginning? I have no idea what you're talking about," she said.

Mandie explained how they had found the steps through the floor of the attic, the treasure in the cellar, and finally the pirate ship's log in the wall of their bedroom.

"So I got the idea to ask Miss Hamby to look up any records she could find on this Jeremiah Grey," Mandie finished.

Mrs. Taft had sat silently, listening to Mandie's explanation. Now she asked, "Do you mean to tell me there is real, valuable treasure in the schoolhouse cellar?" She frowned and added, "And illegal treasure, at that."

"Yes, ma'am," Mandie assured her. "We'll show it to you. We haven't told anyone yet, not even Miss Prudence."

"Of course we'll have to tell Miss Prudence," Mrs. Taft said. "When you girls return to school this afternoon, I'll go with you and talk to her." She turned sideways to look at Mandie and asked, "You are sure this is all for real? I don't want to be made a fool of, especially not in front of Miss Prudence."

"You could go look at all the stuff before we tell Miss Prudence, and then you would know what to say," Mandie suggested.

"Yes, we could, but I believe I'll talk to one of the Heathwood sisters first. I'm sure they will hear I'm at the school and would wonder why I was visiting without seeing them," Mrs. Taft told her.

———

As soon as the noon meal was finished at Mrs. Taft's house, Miss Hamby came with the report she had promised.

When the maid came to the parlor to tell Mrs. Taft that Miss Hamby was at the front door, Mandie's grandmother got up and went to see her. She met Miss Hamby on the front porch.

"I have the report I promised," Miss Hamby said, holding out a stack of papers.

"Thank you very much, Miss Hamby, but since I don't believe in doing business on Sunday, I will accept the report and confer with you when I have read it and will at that time make payment," Mrs. Taft informed her.

"Yes, anytime, Mrs. Taft, thank you," Miss Hamby said, turning to hurry to her buggy standing in the driveway.

Mrs. Taft closed the door and returned to the parlor. She read the report to the girls, but there was nothing in the papers except what Miss Hamby had already told them and a notation she had made that he had no relatives and no descendants. An additional note at the end stated that Miss Hamby had traced a descendant of the missionaries who had been robbed by Jeremiah Grey and would be glad to follow up on that if desired.

Mandie frowned when she heard that and said, "Well, if she found out about this person, why didn't she put it in the report?"

"Because you only asked for the name Jeremiah Grey," Mrs. Taft said with a big smile. "Miss Hamby will expect more money for a report of this descendant."

"Well, I sure wish we knew who it is," Mandie protested.

"Don't worry, dear, I'll get the information when I pay Miss Hamby," Mrs. Taft assured her.

———

Later that day when the girls returned to school, Mrs. Taft came with them. She brought some old clothes in a bag, on the advice of Mandie.

"It's terribly, awfully dirty down there and so is the stuff in the trunks and boxes," she had told her grandmother. "You could change your clothes in our room."

When they arrived at the schoolhouse, Mrs. Taft went down the hallway to knock on the door of the private quarters of the schoolmistresses. Mandie and Celia followed.

"Do come in," Miss Prudence invited them as she opened the door wide.

Once inside and they were all seated, Mrs. Taft told her, "I'm afraid we have a serious problem."

When Mrs. Taft told her what Mandie had related to her, Miss Prudence sat there speechless and could only manage to say, "Indeed."

"Now I have brought old clothes with me and would like to change into these and go down there in the cellar and see for myself exactly what is there," Mrs. Taft added.

Miss Prudence immediately agreed, "Yes, yes, we must go investigate. If you'd like to use my bedroom there." She motioned toward the open door behind her. "And I will change also."

"Thank you," Mrs. Taft said. Rising and turning to the girls, she added, "You two run upstairs and change and get right back down here."

"Yes, ma'am," the girls chorused as they left the room.

When everyone was dressed and ready, Mandie and Celia led the way down into the cellar. Miss Prudence had insisted that they all bring lamps instead of candles in order to see better as they walked across the dark basement.

The girls showed them the old door. They opened it and then pushed some more bricks aside so Mrs. Taft and Miss Prudence could pass through the hole.

Once inside the room, Mandie and Celia anxiously moved from trunk to box to trunk and on around the secret room, as they lifted lids and glanced inside each one. Everything seemed packed full. Mrs. Taft and Miss Prudence were absolutely speechless. Mandie glanced at them and suddenly got a case of the giggles.

"Mandie, this isn't funny, you know," Celia told her as the adults looked anxiously at Mandie.

"I know, I know. I'm not laughing because it's funny," she insisted. "I'm laughing because we managed to beat the old pirate at his own game. We have his loot now, and he thought it was hidden forever."

"For the moment we have it," Mrs. Taft reminded her. "It is not ours to keep. We shall have to do something with all this. I don't know what yet, but something."

Finally Mrs. Taft said she wanted to go to the girls' room to see the ship's log. Mandie cringed as she remembered the terrible hole they had made in the wall. Miss Prudence wasn't going to like that.

But she was surprised. When they got to the girls' room and Miss Prudence saw the hole, she immediately said, "Oh dear, we'll have to find you girls another place to sleep until that hole is repaired, because of rats."

Mandie didn't want to give up their room. "Oh, we aren't afraid of rats. Remember you let me bring Snowball to chase them. In fact, he was the cause of us finding all that stuff," she said.

"Very well, I'll get it repaired tomorrow," Miss Prudence said. "Now shall we inspect the floor in the attic? This house is amazing. I never would have dreamed it held such secrets."

In the attic, the girls explained about the boards, but Miss Prudence said she would get the place opened later to inspect it.

"Oh, we forgot about the ship's log, Miss Prudence, Grandmother," Mandie said as they left the attic. "You looked at the hole, but you didn't look at the book we found in it."

"We'll stop on the way down," Miss Prudence told her.

Back in their room, Mandie and Celia sat quietly while Mrs. Taft and Miss Prudence read the ship's log. And then Mrs. Taft told Miss Prudence about Miss Hamby's report.

"So that is why you girls wanted to visit Miss Hamby," Miss Prudence said, looking at the two. "I certainly wondered about it."

"Yes, ma'am," the girls chorused.

"And we need to find this descendant of the missionaries that she spoke about," Mrs. Taft reminded the schoolmistress.

"Yes, indeed," Miss Prudence agreed.

———

The next day, Mrs. Taft came back to the school after classes and went to show Miss Prudence the report Miss Hamby had given her on the descendant of the missionaries. Miss Prudence called the girls into her office to talk with her and Mrs. Taft.

"According to Miss Hamby's report, the missionary group went out of existence many years ago, and this man, Carl Conover, was only a child when the group broke up. He lives alone down near the depot and picks up odd jobs now and then. He's old and has no relatives that anyone knows of," Mrs. Taft told them.

"And what would you suggest? That we turn all those things in the cellar over to this man?" Miss Prudence asked.

"Well, they belonged to his ancestors, and I don't know of anyone else who has a claim on it," Mrs. Taft replied.

"Grandmother, could we go visit this man?" Mandie asked.

Mrs. Taft looked at Miss Prudence, who nodded and then answered, "Yes, I suppose we could—or should, in fact."

———

Mandie, Celia, Mrs. Taft, and Miss Prudence found the home of the missionary's descendant that afternoon. The house looked old and run down. When they showed up at the old man's door, he was rude to them. "What do you fancy people want?" he asked.

"Are you Carl Conover?" Mrs. Taft asked.

The man looked at her real hard and didn't answer.

"Because if you are Mr. Conover, we have some good news for you," she continued.

The man continued to stare but didn't reply.

Mandie stepped forward, tried to take his hand, but he quickly withdrew. She said, "Mr. Conover, we have some wonderful news for you. We've found the treasures that were stolen from your missionary ancestors when they came to the United States."

He quickly stepped away from her and said, "Got a curse on it."

Everyone looked at each other in surprise.

Mandie continued, "Do you know what we're talking about? The treasures that were stolen off the ship belonging to your ancestors by a pirate named Jeremiah Grey."

"I know all about him. I also figured the treasures were hidden in his house, which is being used for a school now," Carl said. "I don't want anything to do with it. It's got a curse on it. My people died because of it." He shrugged his thin shoulders and squinted his deep-blue eyes.

"But you are the only one we can find connected to this stuff," Mrs. Taft argued. "We have to give it to you."

"No, you don't, lady, 'cause I'm not accepting it. Now you just go back where you came from. I don't want anything to do with it or with you people," the old man insisted.

"All right, then. We'll donate it to some church group," Mrs. Taft said. "But from the looks of this place, I'd say you could use at least some of it." She glanced around the rotten front porch where they stood.

"At least what I've got I earned with my own hands. Now you just go on home," Carl Conover said as he slammed the door shut in their faces.

"Well!" Mandie exclaimed. "Very ungrateful, isn't he?"

"Just overly superstitious, I'd say," her grandmother said.

"And also rude," Miss Prudence added.

"But he did look awfully pitiful and poor," Celia said.

"We'll fix that," Mrs. Taft said. "Let's go make our plans now."

They all went back to the schoolhouse and to Miss Prudence's quarters. It was not yet time for supper, so they discussed what they would do with the treasures.

"If it's agreeable with you, Miss Prudence, here's what we can do," Mrs. Taft began. "I can see Mr. Conover is in bad shape, financially and healthwise. And he won't accept the treasures. There are a couple of pieces I'd like to own in one of those trunks, so why don't I take them and put out the cash value on this Mr. Conover? The balance I think we should donate to some religious group, since that was the kind of people it belonged to. Now what do you think?"

"That is an excellent idea, Mrs. Taft," Miss Prudence agreed.

"But, Grandmother, how are you going to get him to accept anything, money or whatever? He'll figure it's from the treasures," Mandie said.

"We won't have to get him to accept it. We'll just hire some men to rebuild his house, furnish it, stock up some new clothes, and fill up his pantry—and we'll open a bank account in his name with the rest of it," Mrs. Taft explained. "I have an idea he won't refuse any of this."

————

So that's what they did. The girls were allowed to be in charge and they enjoyed every minute of it, most of all when they made a final visit to Mr. Conover's new house, and he actually thanked them.

The girls along with Mrs. Taft and Miss Prudence returned to see him when the work was all done, and this time he invited them inside to sit down.

"I have to apologize," he began, "and I have to admit I didn't like you all, because I thought you all were evidently rich and were down here showing off with all your money and stuff. I know now I was wrong. I've never met finer people, and I thank you all from the bottom of my heart."

Mandie wiped tears of joy from her blue eyes and said, "Oh, Mr. Conover, that's the nicest thing anyone ever said to me."

"And we all thank you," Mrs. Taft told him.

When they got up to leave, Miss Prudence told him, "We want you to know that we'd like for you to come and have dinner with us at the school one day. We'd like for you to see the house the way it is now."

"Oh yes, please do come," Celia said. "We want like you to meet the other girls."

"Well, I thank you all for the invite, but I'm too old to traipse around much anymore. And I want to say I hope you all come back to see me," Mr. Conover told them with a big smile.

"We will," both the girls said as they all left.

On the way back to the schoolhouse, Mrs. Taft told them how much the religious group had appreciated the treasures they had found. "But, mind you, now, all that stuff wasn't gold and jewels. Some of it was fake but it totaled up to quite a sum anyway."

They were in Mrs. Taft's rig, and she insisted they all stop at her house for a cup of tea before returning to school, since it was only midafternoon.

At her house, they found Uncle Ned, who had brought Hilda home. He was sitting in the parlor with her, waiting for Mrs. Taft to return.

"No measles, bring Hilda back," the old man told Mrs. Taft as they all entered the room.

"Yes, thank you, Uncle Ned," Mrs. Taft replied as they sat down.

Mandie walked over to the young girl and said, "Hilda, I'm glad you're home again."

To her great surprise, Hilda started jabbering away in what seemed to be the Cherokee language. Mandie looked at Uncle Ned in astonishment and asked, "Is she speaking Cherokee?"

"We learn Hilda know Cherokee, no English," the old man explained. "Sallie and Morning Star talk to Hilda. Hilda talk back."

"Uncle Ned, do you mean to tell me this child could talk all the time, but she just didn't understand English because she only knew Cherokee?" Mrs. Taft asked.

"Yes, talk all time to Sallie, Morning Star, and also to Dimar," he said, looking at Mandie. "Hilda like Dimar."

"Oh, she's smarter than I am. Here I'm part

Cherokee and don't even know the language. Uncle Ned, I've got to learn," Mandie told him.

"Sallie teach Hilda some English, too," he said with a big smile.

"I'm so glad we finally found out she could talk," Mrs. Taft said.

"Did you come by to see my mother and Uncle John?" Mandie asked.

"John Shaw send word. Number two wife of Jim Shaw claim she got will giving her Jim Shaw's house," Uncle Ned said.

Mandie's heart flip-flopped. "Oh no, she can't have," she said. "I have the will. I gave it to Uncle John, and he was going to get it recorded in the Swain County Courthouse."

"She claim that old will. She got new will," the old man explained. "John Shaw say have courtroom battle."

"Oh dear, that woman is going to cause a lot of trouble," Mrs. Taft said. She looked at Miss Prudence and explained, "We are talking about the woman Amanda's father married after he and Elizabeth were divorced. He was still married to her when he died."

"I'm sorry," Miss Prudence remarked.

"Uncle Ned, did my mother send me any message? I sent her a letter," Mandie told him.

"Only message from John Shaw," Uncle Ned replied.

Mandie frowned and said under her breath to Celia, "Remember I wrote and asked her about going to New York with you and your mother?"

Celia nodded.

"Amanda, we will have to go to Swain County when this thing comes up in court," Mrs. Taft said.

"I do hope it doesn't interfere with your schooling."

"Never mind the schooling, Grandmother," Mandie said. "That woman is not going to take my father's house. It belongs to me, and I'm going to keep it, no matter what I have to do."

As she spoke, she again felt the pain of losing her father. The house was all she had left of her memories. And no one was going to take it away from her. She'd see to that.

Her thoughts turned back to her father and the log cabin at Charley Gap.